Biggles in the Jungle

Biggles in the Jungle

Captain W. E. Johns

Armada

First published in the U.K. in 1942 by
Oxford University Press, London.
This edition was first published in Armada in 1966 by
Fontana Paperbacks,
14 St. James's Place, London SW1A 1PS.

This impression 1981

Printed in Great Britain by
Love & Malcomson Ltd., Brighton Road,
Redhill, Surrey.

Biggles Meets an Old Friend

WITH ITS ALTIMETER registering six thousand feet, a travel-stained amphibian aircraft nosed steadily southward under a Central American sky of azure blue. To port lay the deep green of the Atlantic Ocean, rolling away and away to the infinite distance. To starboard, the primeval forest sprawled like a great stain, filling the landscape until at last it merged into the purple haze of the far horizon. Immediately below the aircraft a white, irregular line of surf marked the juncture of land and sea.

There were three passengers in the machine. At the controls was Squadron-Leader Bigglesworth, D.S.O., better known as "Biggles". In the spare seat beside him, regarding the vast panorama with dispassionate familiarity, was his protégé, "Ginger" Hebblethwaite. Behind, plotting a compass course, sat their mutual friend and comrade, Captain the Honourable "Algy" Lacey. He completed his calculation and came forward.

"I make us out to be off the coast of British Honduras," he announced.

Biggles smiled faintly. "You're a bit late in the day, old boy. Unless I'm mistaken, that's Belize, the capital of the colony, just ahead of us."

"Are you going down?" asked Algy.

"We shall have to," answered Biggles. "That confounded head wind which we ran into this morning was outside my calculations; it lost us so much time that we shall have to fill up with fuel and oil before we go on. This is no place for a forced landing."

"You mean—you'll go down at Belize?"

"Yes. There's a Pan-American Airways maintenance station there. They're a decent crowd. They'll let us have some juice."

"Do you know anybody there?"

"I don't know the Pan-American staff, but I know a fellow in the Government House—that is, if he's still there; a chap named Carruthers. I did him a good turn some years ago, when he was British Vice-Consul at La Paz, in Bolivia, on the other side of the continent. We might look him up. If he's still here no doubt he will be glad to repay an old debt by offering us hospitality. He'll probably be glad to see us in any case; I don't suppose he gets many visitors at an off-the-map place like Belize."

As he spoke Biggles retarded the throttle and allowed the aircraft to lose height in a steady glide that carried it on towards a little town that nestled on the edge of the sea, backed by the sombre forest. He was in no hurry, for—for once—the party was on a pleasure cruise, with no particular object in view beyond seeing something of the world, in fair weather, as an alternative to remaining in London through a dull winter.

Ginger had been largely responsible for the trip. Bored by a spell of inactivity, he had threatened to go off alone, taking the aircraft, an amphibian named *Wanderer*, if the others refused to bestir themselves. Biggles, always tolerant, had proposed a trip to Central America to examine the possibilities of an air service between British possessions on the mainland and the West Indies. This project, he declared, need not necessarily be definitely pursued. It provided an object for the flight, as opposed to aimless wandering.

So far the trip had been uneventful. The adventures which in his heart Ginger had hoped they might encounter had failed to materialise. He was getting slightly bored, and made no secret of it. As a form of relaxation on the ground he had decided to collect butterflies, the beauty of which at some of their ports of call had entranced him, with the result that he was taking a new interest in entomology.

Biggles glanced at him. "Do you know anything about Honduras?" he asked.

Ginger shook his head. "No. I once saw the name on a postage stamp, otherwise I shouldn't have known that the place existed. Is there anything remarkable about it?"

"No, I can't say there is," replied Biggles reflectively. "It's much the same as the rest of Central America. Outside the capital I imagine it's a pretty wild spot. I'm told there's some fine timber there—some of the best mahogany comes from Honduras. The most interesting thing about it from our point of view, having done a bit of aerial exploring, is the Unknown River."

"Unknown River? But that doesn't make sense," protested Ginger. "Either there is a river or there isn't. If there is—well, it must be known. If there isn't, why worry about it?"

"Nobody's worrying about it as far as I know," returned Biggles. "The mouth of the river is known, but from what I can make out the upper reaches have never been explored. It's supposed to rise somewhere in Guatemala, which backs on to Honduras."

"Why hasn't it been explored?"

"Presumably because nobody has had the energy, or the money, or any reason to do so."

"Then why are people concerned about it?"

"Because the river crops up from time to time in the newspapers in connection with the lost Carmichael treasure. There was a talk on the radio about it not long ago."

Ginger started and sat up. "Treasure! Why didn't you say that at first? That sounds more my mark. Tell me about it."

Biggles smiled sadly. "I was afraid you'd get excited if I mentioned the treasure. Don't get any wild ideas—I'm not going off on a treasure-hunt."

"Of course not," agreed Ginger airily. "Still, there's no harm in my knowing about it, is there?"

"I suppose not," assented Biggles. "It's an old tale, not much more than a legend. This country is stiff with legends about treasures. Speaking from memory, this particular yarn started away back in 1860, or thereabouts, when a fellow named Carmichael, travelling up-country, saved the lives of two Indians. In return they promised to show him the spot where Montezuma hid his treasure from the Spaniards. They went, and found a ruined city. Carmichael cut a cross—or made a mark—on a temple, or the ruins of a temple, under which the Indians said the gold was buried; then he came back for help. When he returned he couldn't find the temple—or the city, for that matter. Nobody ever has found it, although they've discovered quite a number of other old cities. The fact is, there are so many of these old cities now swallowed up by the jungle that they can't work out which is the right one. Anyway, most people in Central America have heard of the Carmichael treasure. Several attempts have been made to locate it, but all people find are the traces of a vast and very ancient civilisation—that's all."

A thoughtful look came into Ginger's eyes. "While we're on the spot we might collect what facts there are available," he suggested hopefully.

"To what purpose?" inquired Biggles coldly.

"Well—I mean—of course, I'm not suggesting a definite trip, or anything like that; but if we happened to be near the place——"

"If I have my way we shan't be near it," declared Biggles. "All you'd be likely to find in that jungle would be Indians, mosquitoes, leeches, ticks, snakes, and a few other horrors. If you didn't find them they'd find you. Tropical forests may sound great fun, but they can be very, very uncomfortable. Believe me, I know."

"Does no one ever go into this forest?"

"Oh yes. Rubber collectors and chicle-hunters—mostly natives."

"Chicle? What's that?"

"The stuff they make chewing-gum out of—at least, chicle is the base. Like rubber, it's the sap of a tree. Chicle is the colony's most important export."

Ginger shook his head. "Sounds a sticky business to me."

And there the conversation ended, for Biggles had to

8

concentrate his attention on putting the aircraft on the water. This he did on an open stretch marked by buoys and a wind-stocking pole, which, as he expected, turned out to be an emergency landing-ground for the big Pan-American Clippers that operated up and down the coast from the United States to Argentina. The local superintendent was helpful, giving them a mooring and promising to fill the tanks. Well satisfied with this arrangement, the airmen went into the town to have a meal, seek accommodation for the night, and, if he was still in the colony, call on Carruthers.

As it happened, they met him just leaving his office, and after greetings had been exchanged, and introductions effected, he insisted on their making their home in his roomy bungalow while they were there.

Ginger, although he did not comment on it, was rather disappointed in the size of the town, considering that it was the capital of a British colony. He realised that there was nothing remarkable in meeting Carruthers as they did, for the administration of the colony was carried on by a small staff. Normally, it turned out, Carruthers was senior Resident Magistrate, but at the moment, the Governor being away on leave, he was acting for him. He was a fair, good-looking young man in the late twenties, with keen blue eyes and a closely clipped moustache. His manner was debonair, but behind it was an alert, authoritative bearing.

"You know, Carruthers," observed Biggles, as they sat over their after-dinner coffee, "you've aged a good deal since I last saw you."

"Do you wonder?" Carruthers' tone was rather bitter.

"You mean—it's the climate?"

"Not entirely, although it's certainly enervating. To turn your hair grey, you should try keeping order in thousands of miles of jungle with a handful of men. That's what I'm up against all the time. I know it sounds easy, and you may think I haven't much to do, but believe me, my hands are full."

"How does the jungle make so much work for you?" put in Algy.

"It isn't the jungle; it's the people in it."

9

"Hostile Indians?"

"There are plenty of those, of course, but left alone they wouldn't give us much trouble; but lately they've been playing Old Harry with the up-river stations, and with chicle-collectors and other travellers from the coast. Something seems to have happened. It's almost as if the Indians are organised. In fact, the coastal natives say that is the case, but it's hard to find out just what is going on. There is wild talk—rumour, of course—about a fellow who calls himself King of the Forest, or some equally fantastic title; but what his game is, if he really exists, I haven't yet been able to discover. It's practically impossible to separate rumour from fact. All the same, if half the rumours I hear are true, then there are brains behind the scheme. I'm responsible for the country, so it gets me worried. If anything goes wrong, I have to take the blame."

"But as long as this so-called King of the Forest doesn't interfere with you, what does it matter?" queried Biggles.

"But he is beginning to interfere with me—or somebody is, although I'm still in the dark. For instance, as you probably know, chicle is an important commodity here. It's collected by natives. They are jibbing at going up the river, consequently the stuff isn't coming in as it should. Yet the amazing thing is, there are indications that Honduras chicle is still reaching the U.S.A. in quantities as large as usual. Where is it coming from? Who's collecting it? On top of all this I get an inquiry from the Home Office about three white men who are supposed to have disappeared into the interior. I haven't all the facts yet, but apparently they were on a crazy treasure-hunt."

"Then there is a treasure?" put in Ginger quickly.

Carruthers shrugged his shoulders. "I suppose there must be some foundation for the rumour. It was alleged to have been seen years ago by a fellow named Carmichael. Beyond that I know no more than you do about it. How these three white men got into the interior without official permission, or why they should go without first reporting to me, so that in the event of trouble I should know roughly where they were, I don't understand. They were last heard of on the Unknown River. With two of them I'm not particularly concerned, but the other, a young fellow, happens to have a wealthy and anxious father in the United States, and he's kicking up a nice row because I can't find his son.

"If this fellow who calls himself King of the Forest really exists, and if these Americans have fallen foul of him, they may have had their throats cut. So you see, with one thing and another, I'm having a pretty worrying job. It takes my small staff all its time to handle the ordinary business of the country, without wandering about the jungle looking for lost Americans, chicle-collectors, and self-appointed kings. There is talk of the American archæological survey people coming back here to resume their work. If they do they may be murdered. Yet if I refuse to grant permission there'll be a scream from the Foreign Office."

"What do these people want to do?" inquired Biggles curiously.

"Go on with their survey work—delving into the old ruins that exist in the jungle. As a matter of fact, they've made some very interesting discoveries on the sites of two ancient cities called Tikal and Uaxactun. They now want to locate some more sites which they feel sure exist. It shouldn't be hard, because most of these old cities are marked by pyramids like those of Egypt. They're enormous, and although they are buried in the jungle, the tops are often higher than the highest trees."

"Obviously, what you'll have to do is ascertain if this King of the Forest fellow really exists," declared Biggles. "If he does you'll have to arrest him. You won't have any peace until you do."

Carruthers laughed bitterly. "Arrest him? How? Who is going to find him, for a start?"

"There's no indication of where he hangs out?"

"None. The natives tell a ridiculous story about a secret town in the forest, which doesn't strike me as being likely."

"Still, if that were true, it shouldn't be hard to find."

"You might look for years without finding it."

"In a search from ground level, I agree. I was thinking of reconnaissance from the air."

"That would be an entirely different matter," asserted

11

Carruthers. "Unfortunately, I don't happen to have an Air Force. I can't get a new launch, much less a plane."

Biggles smiled. "I have one," he reminded. "You can borrow it with pleasure."

"Thanks, but who's going to fly it? I'm not a pilot—nor do I know of one in this part of the world."

Biggles took a cigarette and tapped it thoughtfully on the back of his hand. "We're not in a hurry," he said pointedly. "We might find time to have a look round for you—if the idea makes any appeal. There seems to be plenty to look for—pyramids, ruined cities, lost Americans, the king's secret town—treasure—we ought to be able to find *something*. If we did spot anything we could pin-point the place on the map and let you know. That would be a help."

"A help! I should jolly well think it would," declared Carruthers. "Do you seriously mean you'd do this?"

"Why not? We're doing nothing in particular. We might as well do something useful. In any case, although I hadn't mentioned it to the others, I was contemplating a survey flight up the Unknown River, just as a matter of curiosity."

"That would be an important piece of work even if you found nothing else," remarked Carruthers. "I'd really be most grateful if you'd do this."

"Then you can consider it settled," affirmed Biggles.

"Fine. You have official sanction for the undertaking. When do you propose to start?"

Biggles shrugged his shoulders. "It doesn't really matter. As far as I'm concerned I could start tomorrow. If the others aren't too tired——"

"I'm not tired," put in Ginger quickly. "This promises to be interesting. I always did like looking for things."

"Very well. If it's all right with you, Algy, we'll start in the morning," concluded Biggles.

An hour later, to the serenade of bull-frogs croaking in a nearby swamp, Ginger went to bed, to sleep and to dream of kings and lost Americans fighting for a treasure on the summit of a pyramid.

An Unexpected Encounter

A S THE FIRST RAYS of the tropic sun splashed the eastern sky with gleaming gold and turquoise, the thin miasma of mist which hung over the silent lake began to rise, revealing a number of things that floated on its placid surface—a giant water-lily with thick, circular leaves, each as large as a table; over the snow-white blossom a humming-bird, a living ruby with an emerald breast, hung motionless on whirring wings, its three-inch bill probing the nectary for honey; a log, with two protuberances at one end—or what appeared to be a log, although it had a curious trick of submerging and reappearing in another place. There was also an aircraft, an amphibian, which bore on its nose the single word *Wanderer*.

The aircraft rocked gently, so that ripples lapped its sides, as Ginger's head appeared above the central hatchway, to be followed a moment later by the barrel of a rifle. For a brief moment the silence persisted, then it was shattered by a gunshot. The "log" jerked spasmodically, lashing the water to creamy foam before it disappeared. At the sound of the shot a flock of green parrots rose screaming from the nearby forest. Ginger drew himself up level with the hull, regarding intently the spot where the alligator had disappeared.

"Did you get him?" called Biggles from inside the machine.

13

"I don't think so, but I tickled him up a bit," returned Ginger. "It was the same big brute that was nosing round in the night."

Silence returned as Ginger settled himself down on the hull and regarded the forest with keen, interested eyes. They travelled slowly up the mighty trunks of the trees that disappeared out of sight into a canopy of foliage high above; lianas wound round every bole and hung from every bough, passing from tree to tree like a fantastic network of cables. Below, in many places, the ground was strewn with the petals of flowers that bloomed far overhead. Climbing ferns and orchids, too, clung to the trees, sending down aerial roots that added to the tangle. Near the water magnificent tree-ferns flung out feathery fans twenty feet or more in width. Through the maze thus formed swept butterflies, the huge, metallic-blue *Morphos*, and yellow, swallow-tailed *Papilios*. A toucan, with a monstrous red-and-black beak nearly half as big as its body, sat on a branch, but flapped away heavily at the approach of a troop of spider-monkeys.

On the morning following the conversation with Carruthers the *Wanderer* had proceeded up the Unknown River, sometimes flying and sometimes taxiing. Three nights had been spent on the river itself before the lake on which the *Wanderer* now rested had been discovered— a smooth sheet of water that nestled in the jungle a hundred miles from the coast, and the same distance, therefore, from anything in the nature of civilization. It had been decided that the lake would make a good base from which to explore the surrounding country. So far nothing had occurred to interrupt the tranquillity of the cruise, for the *Wanderer* was well equipped with stores and such accessories as were likely to be required.

Ginger called down the hatchway, "Are you fellows getting up?"

"Coming now," answered Biggles.

Ginger grunted, for he was anxious to be off; he could not go ashore because the aircraft was moored some distance from the bank in order to avoid the mosquitoes and other insect pests which were all too plentiful. However, in a few minutes Biggles appeared, and the *Wanderer* was soon surging across the surface of the lake to take off on another survey flight. So far they had not seen any of the pyramids of which Carruthers had spoken, although according to Biggles's reckoning they were in the region of the two ancient cities, Tikal and Uaxactun, where the American Archaeological Society had carried out its excavations.

From the air, the scene presented was one of strange monotony. On all sides, as far as the eye could see, stretched the primeval forest, an undulating expanse of green in various hues reaching to the horizon. In one direction only was it broken. Far away to the west the sun glinted on another lake, which Biggles supposed to be in Guatemala. Not that there was anything to mark the boundary. As in the case of most countries in tropical America, the frontier was assumed to be somewhere in the forest, but it was not possible to say precisely where. The *Wanderer* roared on, climbing steadily.

Presently there was a slight change in the scene, and it became possible to make out areas of open savannah, or rolling meadow-land, although these were often broken by groups of trees and outcrops of rock. Biggles explained to the others that it was generally thought that these areas had originally been cleared by nations that had dwelt there in the past; the jungle, however, was steadily advancing over them again, so that they were fast being swallowed up by the forest.

It was Ginger who first spotted the apex of a pyramid. He caught Biggles by the arm and pointed. "Take a look at that!" he cried.

Biggles cut the throttle and flew lower, so that there was no longer any doubt as to what it was. Near it, two other pyramids, not so high, could just be made out, peeping over the top of the green ocean.

"I should say that's Tikal," observed Biggles.

"I vote we have a look at it from the ground," suggested Ginger.

Biggles, surveying the panorama, noticed a lake nearer to the pyramids than the one they had left, but even so it was some distance away, and he shook his head doubtfully. Flying towards it, however, he came upon another and

15

hitherto unsuspected sheet of water. It was much smaller, and not exactly a lake in the true sense of the word. It appeared rather to be a fairly extensive depression in the ground that had been flooded by a river—probably a tributary of the Unknown River. A stream flowed into it at one end, and out at the other.

"What about that stretch of water?" suggested Ginger. "We ought to be able to get down on it."

Biggles looked dubious. "It's large enough," he admitted. "What I'm afraid of is obstructions. Trees are always falling into these rivers, particularly during the rainy season. If there happens to be any floating about in the middle of the lake, and we hit one of them, we shall be in a mess. We don't know how deep the water is, either. Not that all these hard-wood trees float; if the water is shallow, and there are any lying on the bottom, we shall tear the keel off the boat."

"It looks deep to me," remarked Ginger encouragingly. "Try that patch where there are no water-lilies."

By this time Biggles was within a few feet of the water, leaning over the side eyeing it critically. "All right," he agreed, as he zoomed up to avoid the trees at the far end of the lake. "We'll try it."

Banking steeply, he turned and came back at landing speed. Very slowly, the aircraft sank towards the stretch to which Ginger had referred. There were no visible obstructions. The *Wanderer's* keel slashed the surface of the water, and then sank down with a surging rush that sent ripples racing towards the shore. The machine ran quickly to a standstill.

"Fine!" cried Ginger. "Let's get nearer to the beach—at least, there seems to be a bit of sand over there." He pointed.

Biggles taxied towards it, and brought the *Wanderer* to a standstill with her keel scraping gently on a shelving strip of sandy gravel. "Well, here we are," he announced.

Ginger was about to wade ashore when Biggles caught him by the arm. "Just a minute," he said tersely, staring fixedly at a certain spot.

"What is it?" asked Algy quickly, sensing danger from Biggles's tone of voice.

16

"Can you see what I see—or am I mistaken?" said Biggles quietly. "Just on the edge of the timber, under that spray of crimson orchids."

The others stared.

"Great heavens, it's a man!" breathed Algy.

"Get your guns," ordered Biggles curtly, and, revolver in hand, he stepped down into the shallow water.

The man was lying half in and half out of the forest, his head towards the lake, with one arm outflung as though he had fallen while making a desperate effort to get to the water. That he was a native, or a coloured man, was by this time apparent. He wore only a ragged remnant of shirt and a pair of blue dungaree trousers, also in rags.

"He must be dead," muttered Ginger as they approached.

"I don't think so," returned Biggles quickly. "If he was dead—or if he'd been dead more than an hour or two—he'd be half eaten by this time. There's a hungry army always on the prowl in the forest, looking for meat—and in the water, too, if it comes to that."

Biggles dropped on his knees beside the man and turned him on to his back. He was unconscious. "He's lost a lot of blood," he continued, pointing to an ugly stain on the man's trousers. "Let's see what caused the damage." Taking his knife he cut a slit in the garment so that the wound was exposed. "That's a gunshot wound," he said crisply. "How the dickens did it happen, I wonder? It looks as if there are other people in the forest besides us."

"What on earth would the fellow be doing in a place like this, anyway?" put in Algy.

"I should say he's a chicle-collector—or else a rubber-tapper," answered Biggles. "As I told you, chicle is still collected wild in the forest." He glanced up at Algy. "Get the brandy flask and the medicine chest; we shall have to do what we can for the poor wretch."

He cleaned the wound—a flesh wound in the thigh—and dressed it, while the others, with brandy and water, did what they could to restore consciousness. It did not take them long. The man opened his eyes. Instantly, with

17

"He must be dead," muttered Ginger

a gasp of terror, he tried to get to his feet, but they held him down.

"I wonder what language he speaks," said Ginger.

"If he comes from Belize he'll probably speak English," replied Biggles. "If that fails I'll try Spanish." He said a few words, and as soon as he saw that the man understood he told him that he had nothing to fear.

Together, they got him into a more comfortable position. Ginger, watching closely, noted that the man was older than he had at first supposed; he judged him to be not less than fifty years of age. He had a pleasant if rather wild countenance, and his skin was so dark that he appeared to have both Indian and negro in his ancestry.

Presently the man sat up and regarded his benefactors with incredulous eyes.

"What's your name?" asked Biggles.

The man uttered an unpronounceable word.

Biggles smiled. "That's all right," he told the others. "We'll call him Dusky for short. What are you doing here, and who shot you?" he continued, again addressing the wounded man.

Before Dusky could answer there was a swift footfall near at hand. It brought the comrades round swiftly to face an enormous man who had just emerged from the forest. No one, perhaps not even he himself, could have guessed his nationality; his skin was more white than brown, but it was apparent that he was a half-caste of some sort. Well over six feet in height, and broad in proportion, with a gun over his arm he looked an ugly customer. The only garments he wore were a dirty shirt, open at the throat, and a ragged cotton suit. Nothing more. The lower part of his face was concealed in a tangle of black beard. His eyes were bloodshot and had an unpleasant glint in them. So much the comrades saw in their first appraising glance.

Biggles faced him squarely. Pointing at the wounded man, he said, "Do you know anything about this?"

The stranger took a pace forward, his eyes, heavy with suspicion, darting from one to the other. "What you doing here?" he demanded harshly.

19

"We might ask you the same question," returned Biggles coolly. "Did you shoot this chap?"

For a moment the man did not answer. He glanced at Dusky, scowling, and then looked up again at those who confronted him. For a moment he regarded them reflectively, malevolently.

"What do you here?" he questioned harshly, addressing Biggles.

"Why—have you bought the place or something?"

The scowl grew deeper. "You git out—*pronto*."

Biggles looked surprised. "Are you presuming to tell us where we can go?"

"You git out, or mebbe you don't git out no more," snarled the man.

Biggles appeared to consider the order. Actually, he was wondering if there was any point in staying. It was not as though they had any reason for remaining there.

"What you come here for, huh?" went on the man suspiciously.

"Believe it or not, we're just a picnic party."

The sarcastic leer with which this remark was received made it clear that it was not believed.

"One lake is as good as another to us," continued Biggles. "If you feel that this one is your particular property, we'll pull out. In any case we should have done so, because we shall have to take this man"—Biggles indicated Dusky—"to Belize. His wound needs treatment."

The other started. "No, you don't," he grated.

"But I said we do," returned Biggles calmly.

The man made a significant movement with his gun.

"I shouldn't try that if I were you," Biggles told him evenly. Then, turning to the others, he said, "Get aboard. You know what to do."

Algy nodded, and touched Ginger on the arm. They returned to the aircraft.

Ignoring the stranger, Biggles turned to Dusky. "Do you feel able to walk, or shall I carry you?"

"I can walk, boss." Dusky got stiffly to his feet, standing on one leg.

The man took a quick pace forward as if he would

prevent his departure, but stopped when Biggles turned on him with a crisp, "Stand back! Take a look at the boat."

The man glanced swiftly at the aircraft, over the side of which now projected a light machine-gun of the type known as the "Tommy" gun. For a moment he hesitated, his lips drawn back, showing discoloured teeth; then, turning on his heel, he strode into the forest. An instant later the shrill blast of a whistle rent the air.

"He fetch de others," said Dusky in a panic.

"Get into the boat," snapped Biggles, and taking cover behind a tree, he watched the forest, whence now came answering cries. Not until Dusky had been hauled into the *Wanderer* did he abandon his position and follow him. He was only just in time, for barely had he joined the others when a gang of men, as unsavoury a crowd as could have been imagined, appeared in the gloomy recesses of the forest, running towards the spot. A shot rang out, and a bullet struck the machine somewhere near the tail.

"Get her off," he told Algy, who was already in the pilot's seat. "If we get mixed up in a brawl somebody's liable to be hurt, and then we may find ourselves in the wrong with the authorities."

"Shall I give 'em a burst—just to let 'em know that the gun isn't a dummy?" suggested Ginger tentatively.

"No—we may need our ammunition," answered Biggles.

The last word was drowned in the roar of the engines as Algy started them. The *Wanderer* surged across the water and rose gracefully into the air.

The last they saw of the lake was a crowd of men on the beach they had just left. One, standing in front of the others, was shaking his fist.

"I should be sorry to run into that gang after this," declared Ginger.

"I should have been sorry to run into them at any time," returned Biggles curtly.

"Where shall I make for?" called Algy.

"Go back to the lake—the one we started from this morning," ordered Biggles. "I want to have a word or two with Dusky before we decide what we're going to do."

Dusky Tells His Story and Ginger Learns a Lesson

IT DID NOT TAKE them long to get back to the lake, for on a straight coarse it was not more than forty miles from the scene of their encounter. As soon as the *Wanderer* was safely down preparations were made for a meal, for it was lunch-time, and in any case it was obvious that Dusky was in a famished condition. Little was said until everyone was satisfied, although it was some time before Dusky stated that he had had enough. Ginger made coffee over the spirit lamp while Biggles examined Dusky's wound and dressed it again more carefully.

"It's nothing serious," he announced. "The bullet went right through, so we haven't got to extract it. Luckily it missed the bone. The flesh looks clean enough, so it should heal in a few days."

In making this statement Biggles did not allow for the astonishing recuperative ability of a healthy native, and the wound actually healed at a speed that amazed him. Dusky, possibly because he was accustomed to pain and discomfort, treated it as a mere scratch.

As soon as they were settled Biggles asked Dusky to tell them just how he had come by his wound. Scenting a mystery, he wanted to know about the whole affair.

"Yes, massa, I tell you plenty," answered Dusky eagerly.

"All right; make a start by telling us what you were doing in the forest and how that big stiff got hold of you."

22

"You mean Bogat."

"Is that his name?"

"*Si señor*—Cristoval Bogat." Dusky spoke English with a soft negro accent, curiously broken by odd words of Spanish, a method of speech common enough in Central America.

"I'se chicle-collector, massa," he went on. "Me and my brudders we buy canoe and work for ourselves; take de chicle down de ribber to Belize. One time we do well, den we git scared because chicle-collectors who go up ribber don't come back no more. Den, we ain't go no more money, we make one more trip. We run into dees Bogat men. Dey shoot at us. Dey kill my brudders and capture me, and say me work for dem. Dey make me slabe."

Biggles frowned. "Slave? Do you mean that seriously?"

"Sure I do, massa."

"But slavery was done away with long ago."

Dusky shook his head sadly. "Not up *dis* ribber, massa."

"Which river are you talking about?"

"De Unknown Ribber."

"But we're on a lake."

"Dat so, but de ribber run fro de forest not far away."

Biggles nodded. " I see. Do the authorities know about this slave racket?"

Dusky shrugged his shoulders. "Mebbe. De black trash along Belize talk plenty about it. Mebbe Gov'ment can't do nuthin."

"Who is this fellow Bogat?"

"He sorta right-hand man for de King of de Forest."

Biggles wrinkled his forehead. "King of the Forest? Great Scott! That's an ambitious title. Who is this precious monarch?"

"Ah dunno, boss. Nobody knows for sure. Some say he black man who kill Gov'ment man in Belize and run away; udders say he white man. Dey call him de Tiger. He mighty big boss, and eberyone mighty afraid of him. He boss tousands of Indians and all sorts of men. Dey say he got town up de ribber." Dusky paused.

"Go ahead," invited Biggles; "this is getting interesting. Tell us all you know."

Dusky scratched his short, curly hair. "Der ain't much ter tell, massa."

"Tell us what happened to you."

"Dey capture me and set me to work wid gang ob chicle-collectors. Some gangs dey tap de rubber."

"I get it. And the Tiger gets it all, eh?"

"Sure he does, massa."

"What does he do with it?"

"Ah dunno fo' sure, but dey say it goes out ob de country de udder way, up de ribber and across de mountains."

"That's a pretty state of affairs. The stuff is collected in British territory and then smuggled out of the country, presumably so that the Tiger doesn't have to pay duty on it. Go on, Dusky."

"I work fer a year, mebbe more; I dunno. We slaves all sick wid bad food, and when we can't work dey beat us wid whips. Bogat, he's worse dan de debbil himself. Den one day two white men come. Dey ask ter go see de Tiger. Bogat take dem. Presently dey all together drinking like brudders. After that we don't collect chicle no longer. We made ter go fro de forest to big old spooky city, and dere we dig."

"What for?"

Dusky shook his head. "Nobody knows—nobody 'cept de Tiger and de white men. But we reckon dey dig fer gold. Fust we dig under de old temple——"

"Did you find anything?" put in Ginger quickly.

"Not much. Some silber mugs. Den we go on digging udder places."

"Why did they shoot you?" asked Biggles.

"Becos I run away. I can't stand dem whips no longer, so one night me and some frens, we run, think mebbe we get back ter Belize. Bogat and his gang shot at us— mebbe dey t'ink if we get back to Belize we say what's going on. De udders all get killed or else caught. I get shot too, but I run till I can't run no longer."

"And these friends of yours who were shot—were they all chicle-hunters from Belize?"

"Sure dey were."

Biggles looked at the others. "This is a nice thing," he

24

muttered savagely. "These fellows were British subjects—or at least under British protection. It seems to me that it's high time this self-appointed King of the Forest was shot out of his throne. It must be the fellow Carruthers told us about. I think the thing now is to go down the river and let Carruthers know about this. He may prefer to decide what we ought to do. There is this about it: we now have a useful ally in Dusky, who probably knows his way about this particular stretch of forest."

"The only thing against us going back to the coast is that, as there has been trouble, Carruthers may not want us to come back. He seems to regard all travellers in his province as his responsibility," observed Algy cautiously.

"I'll tell you how we could get over that," declared Ginger. "We needn't all go down the river. If two of us stay here the machine would have to come back to pick us up."

"That's an idea," agreed Biggles. "Algy, suppose you run down to Belize and have a word with Carruthers? The rest of us will stay here. Tell him what we have learned and ask his advice. You could slip down today and come back tomorrow. There's no desperate hurry."

"Okay, if you think that's a wise plan."

"I can't think of anything better. Come on, let's get some stores ashore and make camp. Ginger will have a chance to collect more butterflies while we're waiting."

Thus it was agreed, and shortly afterwards Biggles and Ginger, standing in front of a green canvas tent which they had erected, watched Algy in the *Wanderer* take off and head towards the coast. After it was out of sight they spent some time making the camp ship-shape, stacking the stores and fixing up their hammocks and mosquito nets. Dusky rested quietly in the shade on a waterproof sheet, on a small area of ground which he had burnt to drive away insect pests.

When this task was completed, and there was nothing more they could do, Ginger took his butterfly-net and announced his intention of collecting some specimens. To his surprise, and somewhat to his indignation, Dusky protested, stating with sincere earnestness that this was a most dangerous thing to do. In response to Ginger's demand to be informed in what way it was dangerous, he declared that not only were there many pests, chiefly insect and reptile, in the forest, but there was also great danger of becoming lost. This Ginger found difficult to believe. As far as the pests were concerned, although he did not say so, he held the opinion that these were exaggerated. So far he had seen none except a few mosquitoes. He knew, of course, that such creatures as ticks and leeches abounded, but he felt that these were more likely to prove a source of annoyance than constitute any real danger to a well-dressed traveller.

Biggles did not forbid him to go, but he warned him to be careful. Ginger readily gave his promise to take no risks, and said that in any event he would not go far from camp. He carried a revolver in his hip pocket, and this, he asserted, would enable him to take care of himself. With his butterfly-net under his arm and a killing-jar in his haversack, he set off into the forest.

At first he did not attempt to capture any butterflies, although he saw several, for he was too fascinated by his surroundings. In particular, the humming-birds of many species, all of brilliant colour, occupied his attention. Other birds were less common, although screaming macaws, in gorgeous liveries of yellow, blue and scarlet, occasionally flew overhead. There were also a number of toucans and tanagers, conspicuous in their black plumage with a fiery red blotch above the tail. Occasionally, too, he saw monkeys, but more often was only aware of their presence by the howling they set up as he approached.

At one place, near a pool, he saw numerous butterflies, large blue *Morphos*, and others. Some were drinking; others circled above the pool like a fountain of flowers. He also noted a great variety of wasps, beetles, bees and bugs such as he had never seen before.

He decided that he would endeavour to take some of the butterflies that were hovering over the pool, but he found it difficult to approach from the side on which he stood. Generally speaking, the forest was fairly open, except of course for the festoons of lianas, but between him and the pool there was a screen composed of a lovely creeping plant, with pink and rose coloured blossoms. It grew so thickly as to be impassable.

When just before he had given his word that he would be careful not to lose his way, he had had every intention of observing it to the letter. Not even when he tried to reach the pool did he relax his vigilance, for he turned often to study the trees behind him so that he would recognize them again on his way back. Still taking note of his path, he started to make a detour in order to reach the pool from the far side. In doing this he came to a smaller pool, set in a sylvan glen of breath-taking beauty, and as there were as many butterflies here as round the larger pool, he decided that it would serve his purpose just as well. Forthwith he got busy, and had no difficulty in capturing as many butterflies as he could accommodate. He often took several with one sweep of his net, and afterwards spent some time sorting them out and admiring them. At length, having decided that he had enough, he set about the return journey, observing that he had been rather longer than he intended, for it was beginning to get dark.

It was now—as he afterwards realised—that he made his initial mistake. Some little distance away he saw the curtain of pink creepers that had prevented him from going straight to the larger pool, and thinking to cut off a corner, he went straight towards it. It was not until he reached the flowers, and saw no pool, that he realised that he had been mistaken in assuming that the flowers were those which he had originally seen. However, he was not in the least dismayed, for he could see the curtain of creepers a short distance ahead. Or he thought he could. It was not until he had reached them, and failed to find the pool, that he realised that these groups of creepers were common in the forest.

It now began to rain, and the big drops added to his discomfiture. Giving way to a sense of annoyance, he struck off in the direction in which he felt certain his outward trail lay; and indeed he may have been right; but if so, then he crossed the trail without seeing it. In another five minutes he knew that he was lost. To make matters worse, the foliage overhead was so thick that little light penetrated through it at the best of times; now, already, it was nearly dark. However, he did not lose his head. He did what in the circumstances was the wisest thing he could do. He stood still, and drawing his revolver, fired three shots in quick succession into the air. These were answered almost at once, and he drew a quick breath of relief to know that he was still within earshot of the camp. He started walking in the direction from which the answering shots had come, and this was, of course, his second mistake, although it was a natural one to make. When some minutes had passed, and he still did not meet Biggles, a doubt came into his mind, and he fired again—a single shot. It was answered by the report of a rifle, but it sounded a great distance away. In fact, it sounded farther off than it really was, for he had not yet learned that noises, and even shots, do not carry far in the density of the forest.

After another interval he fired again, but this time there was no reply. It was now quite dark. Angry with himself for behaving, as he thought, like a greenhorn, he decided to make a fire, and with this object in view he incautiously broke off a piece of dead wood from a branch near at hand. A cry of pain broke from his lips, and he dropped the branch as if it had been red hot, for a numbing sensation in the palm of his hand told him that he had been stung. In the darkness he could feel something crawling up his arm. With a shudder of horror he dashed it off. At the same moment another burning pain stung his neck, and he realised that he must have shaken one of the creatures —wasp, ant, he knew not what—off one of the upper branches.

For a minute or two he stood still, getting himself in hand, well aware that at all costs he must not give way to panic. With a soft swish something brushed his face as it flew past, and he broke into a perspiration of fear. The rain stopped, and strange rustlings could be heard in the undergrowth. Once there was a coughing grunt not far away, a sinister sound which could only have been made by a large animal or reptile. Perhaps his greatest horror was that he would accidentally step on one of the snakes with which the jungle abounded.

For how long he groped about in the darkness he did

not know, but what with the pain from the many stings he received from insects and pricks from thorns, he became convinced that he would lose his reason long before dawn. Already he was on the border of delirium, and it was in sheer desperation that he fired his last shot.

To his amazement and joy, it was answered by a shout no great distance away, and presently he saw the glow of a torch coming towards him. It was held by Biggles. Dusky, hobbling on two sticks, accompanied him. He stood still until they joined him, after which Dusky led the way back to camp.

Ginger thought little about his butterflies when he got back, for although he had been in the jungle only a few hours he had been stung all over, and had been pricked by countless thorns. Leeches were clinging to his legs, although these were easily removed. Weak and haggard from strain, he allowed Biggles to put some liniment on his wounds, and then retired to his hammock.

Biggles did not reproach him. "I think you'd be wise to follow Dusky's advice in future," was all he said.

"Don't worry, that was as much of the forest as I want— at any rate for the time being," declared Ginger bitterly.

"Twenty-four hours of that is about as much as any man can stand," Biggles told him seriously. "And now I think we'd better turn in."

A Visitor and a Mystery

IT WAS SHORTLY before noon the following day that the drone of the *Wanderer's* engines announced the return of Algy. He landed, and taxying up to the camp, shouted, "I've brought a visitor! "

Biggles stared, and saw a man in white ducks sitting next to him. "Great Scott! " he ejaculated for Ginger's benefit, "it's Carruthers."

The acting-Governor came ashore with Algy, bringing with him a tall, emaciated-looking man whose skin, yellow from recurrent bouts of fever, seemed to be drawn tightly over the bones. He carried a portfolio.

Carruthers greeted the others warmly, and introduced the tall man as Marcel Chorro, his head clerk.

"So you've run into trouble?" he queried.

"It doesn't seem to surprise you," returned Biggles.

Carruthers shrugged his shoulders. "Why should it? I've already told you that most people do, sooner or later, in this part of the world. If it isn't one thing it's another. But I must admit that you weren't long bumping into it."

"I assume that Lacey has told you what has happened?" asked Biggles.

"Yes."

"Good. Then let's sit down and discuss the matter. I'm anxious to hear your views. Ginger, you might bring something to drink."

30

"Okay, chief."

The party was soon arranged, and Carruthers opened the conversation.

"I think the first point to settle," he began, "is how you fellows feel about this affair. I mean, do you want to stay here or do you want to continue your pleasure cruise?"

"I've got an open mind about it," confessed Biggles. "Frankly, what we do depends largely on your advice. What do you want us to do? You know the country; moreover, you're in a position of authority, so we certainly shouldn't run counter to your orders. How do you feel about things?"

Carruthers sipped his drink and lit a cigarette before he replied. "It's a bit difficult," he admitted. "As I told you, we had heard rumours of the existence of this man who calls himself King of the Forest. There has also been talk of his assistant Bogat; but as for who they are, you know as much as I do. I knew nothing about this slave traffic, or about these excavations that are being carried on. Nor did I know of the coming of the other two white men. I can't imagine who they are."

"They aren't by any chance the survivors of the American party?" suggested Biggles.

"I should hardly think so. Why should they join up with brigands?"

"I take it you'd put a stop to this king business if you could?" questioned Biggles.

"Of course. Really, we ought to stop it."

"Then why don't you?"

Carruthers raised his hands, palm upwards, indicating the forest on either side. "My dear fellow, do you realise how far the jungle extends? You could drop an army in it, and then spend the rest of your life looking for it without finding it. You'd certainly need an army to do any good, and that's something we haven't got here. Think what it would cost to send even a small body of men, with the necessary stores and equipment, on such a job."

"I'm afraid I can't agree with you," returned Biggles imperturbably. "If I had the handling of this situation I shouldn't think in terms of armies. Half of the men would

31

be in hospital most of the time, anyway. This is a job for a small, mobile unit."

Carruthers looked up sharply. "You mean—like your party?"

"Put it that way if you like."

Carruthers rubbed his chin. "Perhaps you're right," he admitted. "All the same, it's quite obvious that you don't know what you're up against. What would you do? How would you start?"

"Clearly, the first thing would be to locate the head-quarters of this gang, and then ascertain just what they're doing. If they're breaking the law—and there doesn't seem to be much doubt about that—then the next step would be either to take them into custody or drive them out of their retreat."

"How?"

"You're going rather too fast. It would necessarily depend upon circumstances. There must be a way of doing it, though. I say that because I have yet to be faced by a problem for which there is no solution."

Carruthers grimaced. "It would be a dangerous business."

"What's that got to do with it?"

The acting-Governor stared hard at Biggles. "By Jingo! I like you," he declared. "I'm afraid we poor blighters who get stuck in the tropics get a bit slack. Seriously, would you, if I gave you the necessary authority, have a look round for me, and make some suggestions as to how we can put an end to this racket?"

"I should think so," returned Biggles slowly. "What do you mean by authority?"

"I could swear you in as special constables, but"—Carruthers laughed awkwardly—"you realise that I've no funds to meet this sort of thing? You would only get constable's pay—three bob a day. All the same, if the affair was brought to a successful conclusion no doubt the finance people at home would refund your out-of-pocket expenses."

"From a financial point of view I shouldn't call that an opportunity to be jumped at," said Biggles, smiling. "The Tiger must be robbing the State of thousands of pounds a year. If I apprehended him and secured a conviction I should expect a bonus."

Carruthers laughed. "Of course, if you did secure a conviction these fellows would get a pretty heavy sentence; they would have their money taken off them, in which case there might be funds to meet your case. Suppose you leave that to me?"

"Certainly. That's good enough," agreed Biggles readily. "I had to raise the point because we're not exactly millionaires. We should have to have a free hand, of course, so that we could go about the thing in our own way."

"Naturally."

"All right." Biggles looked at the others. "That's seems to be all there is to say. We'll see what we can do."

"Splendid," declared Carruthers. "I'll leave the affair in your hands. And now, if that's all, I'd better be getting back to my office. I've plenty to do with the Governor away."

"In that case we'll have a bite, and then I'll fly you back," answered Biggles. "It was good of you to come up here."

"Not at all. On the contrary, I'm obliged to you for your help. Is there anything I can do for you?"

"Yes, there is," returned Biggles promptly. "One of my difficulties is going to be petrol. You see, we reckoned to cruise about always keeping within easy reach of Belize, where we could refuel. My machine has got a pretty useful range, but I've always got to keep enough petrol in the tanks to get back to Belize. That is to say, if I find myself far from Belize I shan't have much margin for cruising, and running up and down to the coast would be an expensive business. Could you send some petrol up to us? If you could send it up the river the boatmen could make a dump somewhere handy."

"I see your point," answered Carruthers. "That can be arranged. In fact, I can send you some right away. There's a small supply at one of our posts not far down the river, for the use of the government launch. I'll send it up by express paddlers. The main supply can follow. Meanwhile, I'll get a message through to our nearest river post for the emergency petrol to be brought up to you. Keep an eye

33

on the river. If you see the canoe coming it might be a good idea to land near it and tell the men where you want the stuff put."

"That's a sound scheme," agreed Biggles. "It will save us a lot of trouble. I take it we can rely on this emergency supply coming? We should be in a mess if our tanks ran low and the stuff didn't arrive."

"Don't worry. I'll see to it," promised Carruthers.

"That's good enough for me," declared Biggles.

And that was the end of the interview. After lunch Biggles flew the acting-Governor back to Belize, where he spent the night, leaving the others in charge of the camp.

He was in the cockpit early the following morning, anxious to get back to discuss ways and means of starting on their new project. Both for safety and simplicity he followed the river—for safety because it offered the only possible means of getting down should engine trouble develop, and for simplicity in that it marked an unmistakable course, and so enabled him to fly yet give his mind to other matters. Fortunately—as it transpired—he cruised along quietly, and there was never an occasion when he found it necessary to turn sharply, or otherwise put a strain on the aircraft. Not that there was anything unusual about this, for Biggles, like the majority of experienced pilots, never, in any circumstances, performed useless stunts.

He was about fifty miles short of his destination, and was on the point of leaving the river for the lake, when he noticed the loose turnbuckle. Just why he noticed it would be hard to say, except that it becomes an instinctive habit for a pilot to keep an eye on everything around him, even though there may not appear to be any immediate necessity for it. His roving eyes, passing over the turnbuckle which braced the flying wires between the starboard wings, stopped suddenly and remained fixed. A second later his left hand slid to the throttle and eased it back; at the same time he moved the joystick forward slightly so that the *Wanderer* began a slow glide towards the river, at this point about a hundred yards wide.

Although to anyone but a pilot it might have appeared a small thing, what he had noticed was this. The turnbuckle should have been screwed up so that none—or not more than one or two—of the threads on the cross-bracing wire were visible. At least six threads could now be seen, and as there were only eight or nine in all, it meant that the entire strain was being carried by two or three threads; even an ordinary strain on the wings might therefore be sufficient to pull the wire clean out of the buckle—which takes the form of a longish, rather fat piece of metal; and since the wings are held in place by these particular wires, should the wires break, or pull out of the turnbuckle, there would be nothing to prevent the wings from tearing off— that is, if one excludes the small fishplates which fasten the roots of the wings to the fuselage.[1]

Now, the turnbuckle concerned was on the starboard side. What made Biggles look at the turnbuckle on the port side he did not know; but he did, and to his alarm, and unspeakable amazement, he saw that the same thing had happened there. His face was pale as he brought the machine down as gently as he could, and a breath of relief broke from his lips as it settled safely on the water. It made him feel slightly weak to realise that the whole time he had been in the air a "bump" might have been sufficient to take his wings off. Once on the water the strain was taken off the wires, and he sat still for a little while regarding the turnbuckles with brooding eyes. When he had first noticed the starboard one he had assumed, not unnaturally, that it had worked loose of its own accord; that it was one of those accidents which can occur to any mechanical device. It should not, of course, be allowed to happen, and since the *Wanderer* was examined every day, it was not easy to see how it could happen. It would have been remarkable enough if only one turnbuckle had worked

[1] The cross bracing wires between the wings of a biplane are called respectively "flying-wires" and "landing-wires". Flying-wires keep the wings of a plane *down* while the machine is in flight; landing-wires hold them up when the machine is at rest. Naturally, when a machine is in flight, the strain on the wings is upward, and the flying-wires hold them down. When the machine is at rest, the strain, imposed simply by gravity, is downward, and it is the landing-wires that hold them up.

loose, but that two should become unscrewed at the same time by accident was incredible. In short, such a coincidence was enough to tax the imagination to breaking point.

Biggles's face was grim as he climbed out on the starboard wing and made the necessary adjustment. The turnbuckle was quite loose, and held the wire by only two threads. It was the same on the other side. Vibration alone might have been sufficient to give the turnbuckles the final twist that must have caused him to crash. Satisfied that they were now in order, he took off and flew over to the lake, where he found everything as he had left it. Algy and Ginger were there, waiting for him.

He taxied to the bank, switched off, and tossing the mooring rope ashore joined the others.

"Ginger, it was your turn yesterday to look over the machine," he said quietly. "You didn't forget by any chance, did you?"

Ginger looked hurt. "Of course I didn't," he retorted hotly. "What made you ask?"

"Only that coming along this morning I happened to notice that the turnbuckles on both flying wires were loose —nearly off, in fact. I had to land on the river and fix them."

There was dead silence for a moment.

"Did you say on *both* wires?" Algy burst out.

"I did."

"Then somebody must have unscrewed them," declared Algy, with such emphasis that he made it clear at once that he was not prepared to accept coincidence as an explanation.

"Yes, I think that's the only answer," agreed Biggles.

"It couldn't have been done here, that's certain," put in Ginger.

"I agree. That means it could only have been done in Belize."

"You didn't put a guard over your machine last night?" queried Algy.

"No. Why should I? What possible reason had I for thinking that it might be interfered with? I shall take jolly good care it doesn't happen again, though."

36

"Somebody must have deliberately tried to crash the machine."

"He tried to do more than that. He tried to kill me at the same time."

"But who on earth in Belize could have done such a thing?"

Biggles smiled faintly. "That's something we may find out presently," he said. "The only possible enemies we can have in this part of the world are those connected with the Tiger, or his pal Bogat; it would seem therefore that the Tiger has friends in Belize."

"That's the only solution," murmured Ginger. "The Tiger's ramifications evidently extend to the coast. Well, forewarned is forearmed, they say; we shall have to keep our eyes open."

"We certainly shall," agreed Biggles warmly. "But come on, we may as well have a bite of lunch; it's too late to start anything today, so we'll get all set for an early move tomorrow. How's Dusky getting along?"

"Fine, he's hopping about already," Ginger answered.

"Did you tell him that we're going to try to put a spoke in the wheel of the Tiger?"

"Yes."

"What did he say?"

"He's flat out to help us," declared Ginger. "He hasn't forgotten that Bogat murdered his brothers."

"Good. I think he's going to be useful," returned Biggles. "Now let's have a bite then talk things over."

The Enemy Strikes

THE UPSHOT of the debate, in which Dusky took part, was this. They would turn in early, and, leaving the lake at dawn, proceed under Dusky's directions to that area in which the headquarters of the Tiger was assumed to be. Whether Dusky would recognise landmarks from the air remained to be seen; on the ground, at any rate, he appeared to have no doubt as to the general direction. Pending this survey, nothing could, of course, be done. As far as they themselves were concerned, the present camp would serve for the time being; if, later, a suitable base could be found nearer to the enemy, then they would move to it. Nothing further could be arranged immediately. This decided, they spent a little while preparing the camp for a more extended stay, clearing the bushes and piling them on the forest side of the tent. At nightfall, with the *Wanderer* moored close in, they got into their hammocks, closed the very necessary mosquito curtains, and went to sleep. There was a short discussion as to whether or not they should take turns to keep guard, but in the end they voted against it, a matter in which they were guided by Dusky, who said that as they were not in the region of savages there was no need for this precaution.

It was therefore with surprise that Ginger awoke some time later—what hour it was he did not know—to find Dusky in quiet conversation with Biggles. He realised that it was the sound of their voices that had awakened him.

Seeing that he was awake, Biggles said, "Dusky swears that there is somebody moving about in the forest."

"Does he mean that he's actually heard somebody?"

"Not exactly. I gather that there have been sounds made by night creatures that indicate that human beings are on the move. He believes that they are coming in this direction."

"But nobody could possibly know that we are here."

"That's what I've told him. All the same, he insists that he's right. You'd better wake Algy."

"Perhaps it's a party of chicle-hunters—nothing to do with us?"

Dusky shook his head. "Not *chicleros*," he announced definitely. "Dey not march at night—too mighty scared."

"We should be foolish not to heed what Dusky says," declared Biggles, starting to put on his clothes. "Wake Algy, and both of you get dressed. We'll go outside the tent and listen. Bring your guns." He himself picked up a rifle and slipped a cartridge into the breech.

Gathered outside the tent, they stood near the edge of the forest, listening intently. A crescent moon hung low in the sky, throwing a broad band of silver across the placid surface of the lake, but within the jungle profound darkness reigned. The air was heavy with heat and the tang of rotting vegetation; vague rustlings betrayed the presence of the invisible army of insects that dwelt in it.

For some minutes the silence continued; then a curious sound came from the forest; it was as though a branch was being violently shaken.

"What on earth was that?" muttered Biggles.

"De monkeys. Dey shake de branches when mens go underneath," breathed Dusky, slightly hoarse with nervousness.

Biggles looked at the others. "This is a funny business," he said quietly. "It's hard to know what to do for the best. Dusky is convinced that somebody is about, but that doesn't necessarily mean that we're being stalked. On the other hand, it may be Bogat's men—whether they're looking for us or not."

"They couldn't possibly know we're here," put in Algy.

"No, but they might guess it. They probably know

39

of the existence of this lake, in which case they might have decided to investigate on the off-chance of finding us here. We're in no case to withstand a serious attack."

"What's the time?" asked Algy suddenly.

Biggles glanced at his watch. "Nearly five."

"It will start to get light in an hour."

Again, out of the forest, came the sinister rustling of branches. A monkey barked, and then broke off abruptly.

Biggles shook his head. "I don't like this. I think we'd better start getting ready for a quick move. You two put the stores back in the machine. Don't make a noise about it. I'll walk a few yards into the forest with Dusky. If I shout an alarm, start the engine."

Twenty minutes passed without further development, except that by the end of that time everything portable had been put on board. Algy and Ginger returned to the edge of the forest, where presently Biggles joined them.

"Dusky was right," he said softly; "I can hear them now, distinctly."

"We've got everything on board except the tent," announced Algy.

"Good—stand fast."

"Where's Dusky?"

"In the forest, scouting."

Hardly had the words left Biggles's lips when Dusky returned; he was shaking with excitement. "Dey come, massa," he panted.

"We'd better play safe until we see how many of them there are," decided Biggles promptly. "Into the machine, everybody. Algy, get ready for a snappy take-off; Ginger, you man the gun, but don't use it until I give the word. Get going."

Not until the others were aboard and the machine cast off did Biggles leave the bank. As he climbed into the aircraft he pushed it a few yards from the shore, leaving it in such a way that the nose faced open water.

"Absolute quiet now," he ordered.

Silence settled again over the scene. The *Wanderer*, plainly visible from the bank, floated motionless, like a great bird asleep. Algy was in the pilot's seat with his hand on the starter, but Biggles and Ginger crouched by the gun, only their eyes showing above the top of the fuselage. The silence was uncanny, and Ginger found it hard to believe that human beings were abroad in the forest, creeping towards the site of the camp. Then he saw an indistinct shadow flit along the fringe of the forest a little way higher up, and he knew that Dusky's woodcraft had not been at fault.

"Here they come," he breathed.

Another figure appeared, another, and another, until at last there were at least a dozen shadowy forms creeping towards the tent. Ginger made out the massive form of Bogat, and nudged Biggles; an answering nudge told him that his signal was understood.

With infinite stealth and patience the outlaws closed in on the tent. Then Bogat, gun at the ready, took the lead and advanced to the flap. He threw it open, and at the same time leapt back. "Come out!" he shouted. The rest raised their guns, covering the entrance.

There was a brief, palpitating interval, then Bogat barked again. "Come out! You can't get away." He naturally assumed the airmen to be in the tent, for after a first penetrating stare at it, he ignored the aircraft.

"Don't move, Bogat; I've got you covered," snapped Biggles. "Do you want something?"

There was a unanimous gasp from the assembled men. Bogat swung round. He half raised his gun, and then, evidently thinking better of it, lowered it.

"I said, do you want something?" repeated Biggles. "If you do it's waiting—a hundred rounds of nickel-coated lead. If you don't want anything, clear out of my camp."

Bogat ducked like lightning, and at the same time fired his gun from the hip.

Ginger's gun spat. He swore afterwards that he didn't consciously pull the trigger; he declared that the shock of Bogat's shot caused his finger automatically to jerk the trigger. Above the uproar that instantly broke out Biggles's voice could be heard yelling to Algy to start up. The engines came to life, and the blast of air flung back by the propellers sent a cloud of fallen leaves whirling into the faces of the outlaws; it also struck the tent and laid it flat. The *Wanderer* surged forward across the water, with

41

Ginger firing spasmodic bursts at the flashes that stabbed the darkness along the edge of the forest. Two or three bullets struck the machine, but as far as could be judged they did no damage. It was impossible to see if any casualties had been inflicted on the enemy. The *Wanderer*, gathering speed, rose into the air.

"Where to?" shouted Algy.

"Make for the river," Biggles told him.

The stars were paling in the sky, but it was still dark. However, this did not worry Biggles, who knew that dawn would have broken by the time they reached the river, so that there would be no difficulty in choosing a landing place.

"We've lost the tent," remarked Ginger angrily.

"But for Dusky we might have lost our lives, and that would have been a far more serious matter," declared Biggles. "We can always get another tent. I must say that I don't like being hounded about by these dagos, but it was a case of discretion being the better part of valour. Our turn will come. From now on it's open war."

Nothing more was said. The *Wanderer* cruised on over the tree-tops. The rim of the sun crept up over the horizon and bathed them in a pink glow. The river appeared, winding like a gigantic snake through the jungle. Biggles took the joystick, and in a little while the aircraft was once more at rest, moored near the bank. The bullet-holes were quickly examined, and it was confirmed that nothing vital had been touched.

"Well, let's have some breakfast," suggested Biggles. "Then we'll move off."

"Move off—where to?" asked Algy.

"To have a look round. What has happened need make no difference to our programme. Bogat has declared war on us, so we know just how we stand."

An hour later the machine was in the air again, heading north-west, following from a considerable height the course of the Unknown River. For the purpose of exploration Biggles would rather have flown lower, but this he dare not risk, for the nearer they flew to the source of the river the narrower it became, and places suitable for landing were fewer and farther between.

For a long time they saw only the same monotonous ocean of jungle, with the jagged peaks of a mountain group cutting into the blue sky far to the north. Dusky stated that the base of these mountains was generally regarded as the boundary between Honduras and Guatemala.

"We may as well have a look at them for all there is to see here," announced Biggles. "I'm beginning to wonder even if there is a city in the forest, whether we should notice it. These confounded trees hide everything. If we can't see anything from the air we might as well pack up. I'm not tackling the job on foot, not for Carruthers or anyone else. When I look at the forest from up here I begin to realize what we're up against. The mountains, at any rate, will be a change of scenery."

Cruising at three miles a minute, instead of—as Dusky assured them—three miles a day; which could be reckoned as normal progress on foot, they reached the mountains in about a quarter of an hour, and from the altimeter it was possible to form a rough estimate of the height. It was necessary to fly at nearly six thousand feet to clear the highest peaks. The jungle persisted for some distance up the slopes, but for the most part the tops were clear of timber, and alternated between stark rock and, in the valleys, grassy savannah. Biggles remarked two or three places where it ought to be possible to land, although without having first examined the ground there would be a certain amount of risk involved.

It was Ginger who spotted the ruined city, although at first he did not recognise it as such. Gazing down on an unexpected plateau, he saw, on the very lip of the steep descent on the southern side, a jumble of rocks of such curious formation that he commented on it.

"That's a queer-looking collection of rocks," he observed casually. "Look how square they are. They might almost be houses."

Biggles stared down at the spot indicated, and as he did so a strange expression came over his face. He pushed open the side window and looked again. "You're dead right," he said slowly. "I'm by no means sure that they're *not* houses."

43

"What!" cried Ginger incredulously. "Let's go down and have a look."

Biggles cut the throttle, and pushing the joystick forward, began to circle lower. Presently the *Wanderer* was flying at not more than a hundred feet above the plateau, and the matter was no longer in doubt. Apart from the shape of what Ginger had taken to be rocks, the regular manner in which they were laid out convinced them all that the work could have been done only by the hand of man.

"By gosh! Let's land somewhere. We must have a look at this," declared Ginger excitedly.

Biggles's eyes were still on the city, around which it was now possible to make out the remains of a wall. "It's deserted," he said. "If anyone was there, he would certainly come out to have a look at us."

As he spoke Biggles studied the savannah beyond the town where it formed the plateau. It was too narrow to be an ideal landing-place, but there was plenty of length, and he decided that with care a landing might be made. He lowered the wheels, made a cautious approach, and settled down to a safe if somewhat bumpy landing.

Ginger was first out. "Come on!" he shouted, starting off towards the ruins. "I shouldn't wonder if the place is littered with gold."

"I should," returned Biggles drily.

Leaving the machine where it had finished its run, they walked briskly to the ruins, for the buildings were no more than that, although it was obvious that at one time the place had been a town of importance. Certain buildings larger than the rest marked the sites of what had once been temples or palaces. The whole place, situated as it was on the edge of a chasm overlooking the southern forest, was in the nature of an eagle's eyrie.

Ginger's dream of gold was soon dispelled. With the exception of numerous broken potsherds, and a bronze hammer which Algy found, the houses—or as many as they visited—were empty.

"I'm afraid we're a few hundred years too late," smiled Biggles. "This place was either abandoned, or sacked, centuries ago. Still, it's an interesting discovery, and archæologists concerned with ancient American civilisations will be tickled to death when they hear about it." He pointed to an obelisk that stood in an open square, carved on its four sides. "That's called a stele," he remarked. "There are any number of them in the forest. That weird-looking carving you can see is writing, but no one has yet learned how to read it. Mind you, I'm only speaking from what I've learned in books."

"You don't think this is one of those old cities where excavations have been going on?" inquired Algy.

"Definitely not, otherwise there would be trenches and other signs," answered Biggles. "This is a new discovery."

"What I should like to know," put in Ginger, "is how on earth the people who lived here got up and down from the forest—or did they spend their lives here?"

"Even if they spent their lives up here, as they may have done after they were driven out of the forest by the people who conquered them, there must have been some way of getting up," replied Biggles. "If we look around we may find it."

It did not take them long to. Walking round the ruined wall, they came to an opening with the remains of an old gate, from which descended a staircase so fantastic that for a little while they could only stare at it with eyes round with wonder. It was partly natural and partly artificial. That is to say, a remarkable feat of Nature had been helped by the hand of man. It was fairly clear what had happened. At some period in the remote past, when the cliff—indeed, the whole mountain—was being formed, the rock, then in a plastic state, had settled down, leaving a narrow projecting cornice running transversely right across the face of the cliff, from top to bottom. The face of the cliff was not smooth, but in the form of gigantic folds, yet the cornice followed each fold faithfully. There were places where it disappeared from sight behind mighty shoulders of rock.

In its original form the cornice had no doubt been extremely rough, and of a width varying from two to six feet, and in that state a mountain goat might well have hesitated to descend by it. Then had come man, presumably one of the extinct nations of America. At any rate, men had worked at the cornice, cutting steps where they were required, so rendering the descent possible; but even so, the path was not one to be taken by a traveller subject to dizziness.

"Jacob's Ladder," murmured Ginger.

Biggles nodded. "It certainly is a remarkable piece of work. I should say that it can't be less than five or six miles from the top to the bottom, following the path, and therefore taking into account the irregular face of the cliff. I remember reading in a book about Bolivia about just such a path on the eastern slope of the Andes. An amusing tale was told of an engineer being paid an enormous salary to superintend a gold mine at the bottom of the staircase; but when he got to it, and saw where he had to go, he not only chucked up the job but declared that he wouldn't go down the path for all the gold in South America."

"I don't blame him," remarked Algy feelingly. "I'd hate to go down this one."

"Oh, I don't know; it isn't as bad as all that," returned Biggles. "After all, some of the corniche roads in the Alps are pretty grim, and people who live in the mountain villages have to go up and down them constantly."

"It must have been a colossal task, cutting those steps," put in Ginger.

"The ancients apparently liked colossal tasks," replied Biggles. "What about the pyramids of Egypt, and the Great Wall of China? This is nothing compared with them."

At this juncture, Dusky, who had so far remained silent, interrupted with the surprising statement that he had seen the bottom of the stairway. Interrogation elicited the information that while he had been working for Bogat, clearing undergrowth from the ruins in the jungle near the foot of a cliff, he had come upon just such a flight of steps leading upwards. Asked by Biggles if he had revealed this discovery to Bogat, he said no, the reason being that, although he did not know where the steps led, he thought they might one day provide a means of escape. He had made the discovery about six months ago, as near as he could judge.

"Well, I must say it seems highly improbable that there can be two such stairways," remarked Biggles. "In that case, if we followed these steps we should come out either in, or very near, the excavations where the Tiger and the two white men are working. When you think about it, that is not altogether surprising; in fact, it seems quite a natural thing that there should be a town at the foot of these steps as well as at the top."

"The question that seems to arise in that case is, has the Tiger discovered the staircase since the time Dusky was working at the bottom?" put in Algy.

"I should say not," answered Biggles without hesitation. "If the Tiger had discovered the steps he would most certainly have come up here, and even if he didn't start excavating—as seems probable—he would surely have left some traces of his visit:—old tins, or ashes of the fires where he did his cooking."

"Yes, that's reasonable," agreed Algy. "What it comes to, then, is this. If Dusky's supposition is correct, we have discovered a way down into the Tiger's camp."

"That's it," nodded Biggles.

"What are we going to do?" queried Ginger eagerly. "I'm all in favour of doing a bit of exploring up here on our own account."

"We might have time to do that later on, but at the moment, since our stores are not unlimited, I think we owe it to Carruthers to stick to our job."

"You mean—go down the steps and try to get hold of the Tiger?"

"What else?"

Ginger looked at the stairway and drew back, shuddering. "Strewth! I'm not so keen on that. I don't mind looking down from a plane, but to crawl down that dizzy path, with all that way to fall if we miss a step, doesn't strike me as a jaunt to be undertaken lightly."

"Oh, that's all right," replied Biggles calmly. "All the same, I'm not entirely happy at the idea of all of us going. Somebody ought to stay to look after the machine. Apart from that, if we got in a jam going down we should all be in the same boat, whereas if somebody stayed behind he might be able to help the others."

"That's sound reasoning," murmured Algy.

"I'll tell you what: let's compromise," decided Biggles. "Algy, you and Dusky stay up here to keep an eye on things. Ginger and I will do a bit of exploring. If we find it's easy going all the way down we'll come back and let you know; on the other hand, if we find we can't get down, we shall have to come back anyway."

"Good enough," agreed Algy. "When are you going?"

"Right away. There's no need to wait until tomorrow."

"What about kit?"

"We'll take a tin of bully and some biscuits, a water-bottle and our rifles. That ought to be enough—for the first trip at any rate."

This being agreed, the party returned to the machine, where the necessary kit was obtained and a meal taken. They then returned to Jacob's Ladder. Biggles, with his rifle slung on his left shoulder, started down. Ginger, after a deep breath, followed.

Down the Unknown Trail

FOR THE FIRST hundred steps Ginger's head swam to such an extent that he felt sick and dizzy; more than once he had to halt and lean weakly against the sheer wall of the cliff that rose up on the right-hand side of the path, hardly daring to look at the frightful void that fell away on his left. In places the cliff was more than sheer; owing to faults in the rock, the path had been dug so far into it that the wall overhung the steps. There were places, too, where the path projected over the abyss in the manner of a cornice, so that one false step would mean a drop of four thousand feet or more to the forest. A slight heat haze hung over the tree-tops, making them look farther away than they really were; it also gave the forest an atmosphere of mystery, and created an impression of looking down upon another world. Thus, thought Ginger, might a man feel descending to Earth from another planet.

Biggles appeared to be little troubled by the terrifying drop. He strode on, rifle on his shoulder, whistling softly, and stopping only to warn Ginger of bad places, places where the wind and rain had worn the steps away so that no more than a smooth, narrow projection remained.

However, one becomes accustomed to anything, and after the first hundred yards Ginger began to breathe more freely. Once, while Biggles was waiting for him, he remarked, "What would happen if we met somebody coming the other way? I should hate to try to pass anybody."

Biggles laughed softly. "I don't think we shall meet anyone on this path," he observed lightly. "Save your breath; we shall need it coming back."

They went on. Condors appeared, stiff-winged, looking as big as gliders; they circled slowly, their heads turned always to face the invaders of their domain. Ginger eyed them nervously.

"We should be in a mess if they decided to attack us," he said anxiously.

"So would they," answered Biggles briefly, tapping his rifle.

Rounding the shoulder of rock that up to now concealed what lay beyond, they stopped for a moment to admire the stupendous view that unfolded before them; it seemed that the very world was at their feet. The path, after cutting into a colossal gorge, reappeared again on the far side, five hundred feet below; a mere thread it looked, winding down and down interminably. For the first time Ginger appreciated the full length of it.

"I shouldn't think the people who lived up top were ever invaded," he opined. "Why, a couple of men could hold this path against an army."

"Easily," agreed Biggles. "I'd rather be the man at the top than one of the fellows coming up."

After that, for an hour they walked on with hardly a word. The heat flung down by the sun, and radiated by the rock, always intense, became worse as they descended. As Ginger remarked, it was like going down into a furnace.

They were nearing the bottom—at least, they were more than three-quarters of the way down—when the steps ended abruptly in a veritable chaos of rock. At first Ginger thought they had reached the foot of the stairway, but Biggles pointed out that this was not so, and investigation soon proved his theory, which was that in the remote past a landslide had fallen across the path, carrying a section of it away.

"If we can find a way across this mass of detritus we ought to strike the steps again on the other side," he declared. "We know that the steps go right down to the forest, because Dusky saw them there."

"Yes, of course," answered Ginger.

"All the same, anyone coming up the steps, encountering this pile of debris, might well think that they had come to the end of the stairway," resumed Biggles. "Unless they persevered, and forced a way across the landslide, they would not know that the steps continued and went right on up to the top. Let's push on. Be careful where you're putting your feet, because some of this stuff doesn't look any too safe. If we started a movement the whole lot might slide again. Come on—this seems to be the easiest way."

Biggles proceeded, choosing his path carefully, with Ginger following close behind. From his point of view there was now at least one advantage: there was no longer the precipice to fear, for the route Biggles had chosen traversed the landslide.

And so they came upon the village. It was entirely unexpected, for there had been absolutely nothing to indicate its presence. Reaching the bottom of a steep incline, across a confused jumble of mighty boulders, they found themselves confronted by a drop of some thirty or forty feet into a pleasant valley which the giant forest trees had failed to cross. That is to say, the valley marked the top limit of the big timber. Trees could be seen on the far side, and these, presumably, went right on down to the forest proper. There were no trees on the side where they stood regarding the scene. Nor were there any big trees in the valley, which was carpeted with verdant grasses and flowering shrubs. Up the centre of it ran a wide track, ending at a modern village. Actually, it appeared to be something more than a village, although they used the term for want of a better one. In the centre of a fairly extensive group of ramshackle buildings stood a fine bungalow, well built of heavy timber. At the back of it, and evidently a part of the premises, was a range of outbuildings roofed with corrugated iron. Radiating from this centre were rows of small houses. From a courtyard between the bungalow and the outbuildings smoke was rising lazily into the air from an outside cooking stove. A woman, conspicuous with a scarlet handkerchief tied round her head, did something at the fire and then disappeared into the house. Apart from some mules grazing higher up the valley, which appeared to end abruptly, there was no other sign of life.

As soon as Biggles and Ginger came in sight of this utterly unexpected feature they stopped, and after a few seconds' incredulous contemplation of it, sat down abruptly.

"Great Scott!" Biggles muttered. "What the deuce is all this?"

Ginger, squatting beside him, answered, "Don't ask me."

Biggles regarded the village thoughtfully. "There's only one answer," he said slowly. "The Tiger would never tolerate a second gang in the same area, so this must be part of his organisation. If that is so—and I'm convinced I'm right—then this might even be his secret retreat: the place Dusky spoke about. The fact that there are women—or at least one woman—here, proves fairly conclusively that this is a permanent settlement. The big house proves it, too, if it comes to that."

"So what?" inquired Ginger. "We should be taking a chance if we tried to cross that valley. There must be others here besides that woman we saw. We should be spotted for a certainty."

"We may not have to cross the valley," answered Biggles. "I have a feeling that this is our objective."

Ginger started. "What do you mean—our objective?"

"Well, we were only going to the bottom of the stairway in order to locate the Tiger's headquarters. There was no other purpose in our going down. That bungalow, unless I am mistaken, is the palace of the King of the Forest, so there is no need for us to go any farther."

"What are you going to do—go back and let Algy know what we've found?"

"I don't think so—not for the moment, anyway. We should only have to come down again."

"If Carruthers and his police were here we could raid the place," murmured Ginger.

"Quite, but they don't happen to be here. In any case, there wouldn't be much purpose in raiding the place if the Tiger wasn't here. He's the man we want—he and Bogat. Unless they were captured the racket would still go on."

Ginger shrugged his shoulders. "Well, you're the boss. What's the plan—or haven't you got one?"

"There's only one thing we can do, as far as I can see," replied Biggles, "and that's have a look round the village while we're here, while the place is comparatively deserted. We may not get another such chance. Don't forget that so far we have no actual proof of what the Tiger is doing—that is, proof that would carry weight in a court of law. It wouldn't be any use just talking vaguely about the Tiger being a crook, a slave-driver, a chicle thief, without evidence to prove it. This may be our chance to get such evidence. I'm going down into the village."

Ginger stared aghast. "Going down! You must be crazy."

"We shan't collect any evidence sitting here."

"We could watch them, though, and spot what was going on."

"Even so, I can't see that we should learn more than we already know. We must get some concrete proof to secure a conviction. All the same, if we could capture the Tiger, or Bogat, and get back to the coast, we might hold him until we'd obtained the proof we need. Perhaps some of the slaves would give evidence. But we shan't get any of these things sitting here. I'm going down."

"What do you want me to do? Shall I come with you, or stay here?"

Biggles thought for a moment. "I think you'd better come with me," he decided. "I may need a witness if I find anything—otherwise I should only have my unsubstantiated word."

"Suppose things go wrong? Algy won't know what's happened to us."

"We can easily get over that."

Taking his notebook from his pocket, Biggles tore out a page and scribbled a brief message to the effect that a village was in the valley just ahead, and they were going down into it. Returning to the stairway, he put the message under a stone in a conspicuous place, and built a little cairn beside it so that it could not be missed by anyone coming down. This done, they returned to the valley, and

53

after hunting about for a little while found a way down into it.

"Keep this place in your mind's eye," said Biggles quietly, surveying the spot where they had descended. "We may have to come back this way—in a hurry. Try to get a mental photograph of the silhouette of the rocks, in case we have to find it in the dark."

This did not take long, after which Biggles turned towards the village.

"I think our best policy is to go straight up to the house," he surprised Ginger by saying. "In fact, I don't see that we can do anything else. There's no real cover, so even if we tried stalking tactics it is almost certain that we should be seen; and if we were spotted skulking like a couple of thieves, there would probably be an outcry. I think this is a case for bluff. All the same, we needn't expose ourselves unnecessarily; we'll just stroll along, and if nobody sees our faces we may get away with it."

"You know best," agreed Ginger, "but it seems a risky business to me. I never was one for jumping into a lion's den without first making sure that the lion wasn't at home."

Biggles smiled, and walked on towards the village, the nearest buildings of which were not more than a hundred yards away.

They had covered about half the distance when Biggles touched Ginger on the arm, and with an inclination of his head indicated something that he had seen. The boundaries of the valley were now apparent. Hemmed in by cliffs, sometimes high, and, in a few places, fairly low, such as at the spot where they had entered it, there was only one proper entrance. This was a narrow pass at the southern end of the track, a mere defile through the rock wall, presumably where those who lived in the village descended to the forest some four hundred feet below. At this natural gateway two men were on guard; at least, they were armed with rifles. Smoking, they lounged against the wall of the pass.

"If that is the only entrance to the valley, those fellows will wonder how the deuce we got in," said Biggles softly. "There is this about it, though: the people in the village—if

54

there are any—knowing that men are on guard at the entrance, might suppose that we are here on business. My word," he went on, glancing round, "what a spot for a hide-out. Carruthers was right. An army might have wandered about in the forest for years without even suspecting that this place was here. It would need an army to capture it, too, against a score of determined men."

"There's one thing that puzzles me," remarked Ginger. "Dusky said he found the foot of the stairway. Anyway, he saw a stairway, so we must assume that it was the terminus of the path we came down. Yet, judging by the way he mentioned it—he was actually clearing the jungle, you remember?—it seems that those steps weren't used, which means there must be another way up. In fact, the Tiger may still not know that Dusky's stairway exists."

"By jove! I didn't think of that," returned Biggles quickly. "You're dead right. Whether they have known about the stairway all along, or discovered it since Dusky was there, it seems unlikely that it is used. There is probably an easier way down. It doesn't matter at the moment, but we'll bear it in mind."

By this time they had reached the village, still without seeing anyone apart from the two men on duty. A drowsy silence broken only by the hum of insects hung on the air. Biggles avoided the main street, a dusty track often interrupted by outcrops of rock, which wound a crooked course between the houses—most of them little better than hovels—and kept to the rear of the buildings, moving steadily towards the big bungalow. As they neared it they came suddenly upon a woman; she was on her knees, grinding maize; she looked surprised when she saw the strangers, but said nothing, and after they had passed they could hear her going on with her monotonous task.

"It would be a joke, wouldn't it, if this isn't the place we're looking for, after all?" murmured Ginger. "It might turn out to be a perfectly legitimate village."

"People don't post guards at the entrance to a perfectly legitimate village," Biggles reminded him. "Moreover, if this place was above-board, there would surely be some attempt at cultivation; and there would be no need for *chicleros* to sweat up and down four hundred feet of rock

55

every time they went to work. All right—here we are; keep quiet now."

They had reached the entrance to the yard that gave access to the outbuildings of the big house, the back door of which also opened into it. The fire which they had seen from the rocks was still burning; above it was suspended an iron cauldron from which arose an appetising aroma.

"We'll try the outbuildings first," said Biggles quietly, and walked over to them; but if he hoped to see what they contained he was disappointed, for they were locked, every one of them, and there were six in all, large and small. But from the far one they were granted a view of something which hitherto had been hidden by a corner of the house. It was a garden, a walled-in area, an unsuspected Eden. Grapes hung in purple clusters from an overhead trellis; scarlet tomatoes gleamed among the golden stalks of Indian corn; huge yellow gourds lay about among vines that wandered through flowers of brilliant colours. A bush loaded with great blue plums made Ginger's mouth water. This pleasant scene was enhanced by a pigeon-cote, where several birds were preening thmselves. Into this unsuspected paradise Biggles led the way. Ginger made for the plums, but Biggles dragged him back into a shady arbour where a tiny fountain bubbled.

"Don't be an ass," he muttered; "we're on thin ice here. Don't you realise that we're in the king's garden? Stand fast."

Peering through the creepers that covered the arbour, Ginger saw that they were now at the side of the house. A long, low window overlooked the garden. Near it was a door. It was open.

"We're doing well. Let's have a look inside," murmured Biggles, and went on to the door, which gave access to the garden, but obviously was not the main entrance to the house. After a cautious peep inside Biggles took a pace over the threshold, Ginger at his elbow. He whistled softly as he looked around.

"And I should say this is the king's parlour," he whispered.

The room was magnificently, if ostentatiously, furnished as something between a lounge and an office. An old, beautifully carved Spanish sideboard was disfigured by a lot of cheap, modern bric-à-brac. Bottles and glasses stood on a brass-topped table. A modern roll-top desk, littered with account-books and papers, stood near the far wall; but the piece that fascinated Ginger most was a fine, leather-covered chest. In strange contrast, near it stood an American steel safe. A second door led into the interior of the house. A strange foreign odour hung in the sultry air.

So much the visitors saw at a glance. After listening intently for a moment, Biggles walked over to the desk, where he began to scan the papers, but without disturbing them. He opened a ledger, and whistled softly as his eyes ran down the items.

"This is all we wanted to know," he breathed. "This is the Tiger's sanctum all right, and these are his accounts. There's enough documentary evidence here to hang him twice over. He's evidently a gentleman of some taste, too. Hullo, what's this?"

As he spoke Biggles picked up a tiny slip of flimsy paper that was lying on the desk, held in place by a cartridge used as a paper-weight. As he picked up the paper and read what was written on it his brow creased with anger and astonishment; he stared at it for so long that Ginger's curiosity could not be restrained.

"What is it?" he demanded.

"You might well ask," replied Biggles through his teeth. "It explains a lot of things. Take a look at that." He passed the paper.

Ginger read the message, his lips forming the words:

"Keep watch for three Britishers in airplane. They are government spies sent to get you, acting for Carruthers. Names are Bigglesworth, Lacey and Hebblethwaite. They have been sworn in as police, and have got one of your peons, the man Bogat shot. They will use him as evidence.

"M. C."

"Did you note the initials?" inquired Biggles.
"Yes. Who on earth——"

"M.C. stands for Marcel Chorro—who else? He's the only man besides Carruthers who knows what we're doing. Evidently he is one of the Tiger's spies. My goodness! No wonder Carruthers found it hard to get evidence. Chorro must have been the swine who loosened my turnbuckles—yes, by gosh! Now we know how Bogat knew we were camping at the lake. He marched straight through the forest to attack us."

"But how the dickens could Chorro have got a message through in the time?" gasped Ginger. "The fastest canoe on the river couldn't get here much inside a week."

"You saw the pigeon-cote outside, didn't you? Notice the thin paper used for the message."

Ginger caught his breath. "So *that's* it. Chorro and the Tiger run a pigeon post."

"Undoubtedly. Come on, we've seen enough. It's no use tempting providence—we'll get back to Algy right away."

Biggles started towards the door, but recoiled in horror. With staring eyes he clutched Ginger by the arm and held him back.

Ginger, following the direction of Biggles's eyes, felt his blood turn to ice. For some minutes he had been aware that the strange aroma had been getting more noticeable, now he saw the reason.

Emerging slowly from the chest that he had so much admired was a snake, but such a snake as not even a nightmare could have produced. As thick as a man's thigh, coil after coil was gliding sinuously out of the chest as though it would never end. Already fifteen feet of rippling horror lay stretched across the room, cutting them off from the door and the window.

In the Claws of the Tiger

HOW LONG Ginger stood staring at the snake he did not know. He seemed to lose all count of time; he forgot where he was, and what he was doing. He was conscious of one thing only—the snake. Its little black eyes, glinting like crystals when the light caught them, fascinated him. After the first gasp of horror not a sound left his lips.

Pulling himself together with a mighty effort, he looked at Biggles, and saw that he, too, was at a loss to know what to do. He stared at the snake, then at the door, then back at the reptile. Once he braced himself as if he contemplated taking a flying leap; then he cocked his rifle and tried in vain to draw a bead on the swaying head.

"Go on—shoot," urged Ginger, in something very near a panic.

"I daren't risk it," muttered Biggles. "That head is a small mark for a rifle, and if I miss, the shot will raise the place. If I only wounded the beast goodness knows what would happen."

Curiously enough, the snake—which Biggles thought was a python—made no attempt to attack them; it lay across the floor, watching them in an almost human manner; it was as if it knew they were intruders, and had determined to prevent them from escaping. Every time they moved, it raised its head, hissing venomously, causing them to retire.

Torn by doubt and indecision, Biggles was still trying to

think of a way out of their quandary when from outside came the sound of voices, followed a moment later by the trampling of footsteps; and almost before he was fully alive to their danger the inner door was thrown open and a man came in to the room. He took one pace only and then stopped dead, staring at the spectacle that confronted him. Then his hand flashed to a holster that was strapped to his hip, and came up holding a revolver.

At first Ginger thought he was going to shoot the snake, but it was soon clear that this was not his intention, for he took not the slightest notice of the creature, although it had turned towards him and was now rubbing its sinuous body against his leg. Not until then did Ginger realise that the reptile was a pet, and not a wild creature that had invaded the house from the forest.

The newcomer, who was clearly the owner of the house, even if he were not the reputed King of the Forest, was a striking figure, but certainly not a pleasing one. He was a half-caste, the black predominating, of about fifty years of age; he was of medium height, but of massive, though corpulent, proportions. His arms and shoulders might have been those of a gorilla, but as an example of physique he was spoilt by a paunch of a stomach which, like his face, was flabby from over-eating or self-indulgence, or both. His cheeks were puffy, but his chin was pugnacious. His eyes were small and dark; they were never still, but flashed suspiciously this way and that. His hair was long and luxuriant, but had an unmistakable negroid twist in it. An enormous black moustache drooped from his upper lip. He was dressed—or rather, over-dressed—in a uniform so elaborate, so heavy with gold braid, and of colours so brilliant that not even a cinema commissionaire would have dared to wear it. The general effect was that of a comic-opera brigand; but, looking at the coarse face, Biggles judged him to be a man of considerable mental and physical strength, vain, crafty, and unscrupulous; a man who would be brutal for the sheer pleasure of it, but who, at a pinch, might turn out to be a coward.

The newcomer broke the silence by calling out in a loud voice, "Marita! Who are these men?" He spoke in Spanish.

A woman, evidently Marita, she who had tended the

His hand flashed to a holster, and came up holding a revolver

fire, appeared in the background. In the same language she answered, nervously, that she did not know the men. She had never seen them before—which was true enough.

The man came farther into the room. He spoke in a soft, sibilant voice to the snake, which writhed out of sight under the desk. Then he eyed Biggles suspiciously.

"What language you speak, eh?" he asked, talking now in English with an American accent, from which it may be concluded that he assumed the airmen to be either British or American.

"We speak English," answered Biggles.

"What you come here for, huh?" rasped the half-caste. Then, before Biggles could answer, understanding flashed into his eyes. They switched to the desk, and Biggles knew that he had remembered the note from Chorro.

"Am I right in supposing that I'm speaking to the King of the Forest?" inquired Biggles calmly.

The half-caste's eyes narrowed. "I am the king," he said harshly. "Where is the other man?"

"What other man?"

"There are three of you. Where is he?"

"What are you talking about?" demanded Biggles, although he knew well enough what was meant.

"Which of you is Bigglesworth?"

Biggles realised that it was useless to pretend. The Tiger knew they were in the district; he was also aware that the chances of any other white men being there were so remote as to be ignored.

"I'm Bigglesworth," answered Biggles quietly.

An ugly smile spread slowly over the Tiger's face. He put a small silver whistle to his lips and blew a shrill signal. Instantly men came running. With them were two white men whom Biggles guessed were those to whom Dusky had referred. The first was tall and cadaverous; he could only be called white by courtesy, for jaundice had set its mark on his face, leaving it an unhealthy yellow. The same unpleasant tint was discernible in the whites of his eyes, which were pale grey and set under shaggy brows. His mouth was large, with thin lips; nor was his appearance improved by ears that stuck out nearly at right angles from his head. His companion was a weedy-looking individual of nondescript type. Lank, hay-coloured hair covered his head; a moustache of the same tint straggled across his upper lip, stained in the middle with nicotine. An untidy, hand-made cigarette was even then in his mouth.

The Tiger called them in and indicated the prisoners with a theatrical wave of his arm. "The cops got here before us—that saves us the trouble of going to fetch them." Then a look of doubt returned to his eyes. "Where's the other one?" he purred.

"Oh, he's about," returned Biggles evenly.

"Where is he?"

"Look around, maybe you'll find him . . . maybe not."

The Tiger changed the subject. "How did you get here? Who brought you?"

Biggles smiled faintly. "We brought ourselves."

"That's a lie," snarled the Tiger, crouching as though to spring, and Biggles began to understand how he had got his doubtful nickname. "Somebody showed you the way in—who was it? I'll tear the hide off him."

"Sorry," said Biggles, "but that's a pleasure you will be denied, for the simple reason that no such person exists."

"How did you get past the guards?" The Tiger seemed to be genuinely worried by the fact that strangers had penetrated into his retreat.

"Oh, they were looking the other way," returned Biggles truthfully.

The expression on the Tiger's face boded no good for the sentries, but Biggles was not concerned about their fate.

"Take them away," snapped the Tiger.

Several men, a rag-tag but nevertheless picturesque set of ruffians, stepped forward and disarmed the prisoners. They offered no resistance, knowing it to be useless.

"What shall we do with them, your Majesty?" fawned the man who appeared to be in charge.

Biggles smiled at the words "your Majesty." It seemed that the title of King was actually enjoyed by the Tiger among his subjects.

63

The Tiger considered the prisoners reflectively; then a smile crept over his face. "Put them next to Juanita; she must be getting hungry," he ordered. "When we get the other we will lift the bar and leave them together. All right; take them away."

Rough hands were laid on the prisoners. Biggles did not protest, perceiving that with the man with whom they had to deal it would be a waste of time. No doubt he had already been responsible for the death of scores of wretched slaves, so another murder, more or less, would not affect his conscience. In any case it was obvious that he thought himself safe in his secret retreat.

As they were marched towards the outbuildings, Ginger wondered who Juanita was, although that she was something unpleasant he had no doubt whatever. He was soon to learn. A door was opened, and they were pushed inside a shed. The door slammed, and a heavy bar crashed in place.

After the dazzling sunshine outside it seemed to be pitch black within, but as his eyes grew accustomed to the darkness Ginger began to make out some of the features of their prison. The first thing he saw was Biggles standing beside him, also peering about; next, a row of stout vertical bamboo bars that separated them from another compartment. This second stall had another barred wall, or part of a wall, beyond which was the open air. It needed no second glance to see that it was, in fact, a cage. Perhaps a better description would be to call the whole place a cage, divided by bars into two compartments. They were in one part. But what was in the other? Ginger looked for the occupant —for he knew that there must be one—but in vain. If proof that they were not alone were needed, a menagerie-like stench of wild beast provided it. Then he saw a small hole at the back of the next compartment, and he looked no farther; he knew that the beast, whatever it was, was inside, in its lair.

Biggles put a hand on the partition, and shook it. "This is the bar the Tiger meant when he spoke about lifting it," he remarked. "Juanita is on the other side. Apparently, when feeding time comes, the partition is raised from the outside, leaving us all together."

64

Algy Explores

ALGY SPENT SOME TIME loafing about the ruined village, but as the day wore on, and Biggles and Ginger did not return, he became conscious of an uneasiness which presently turned to anxiety, and he took up a position at the top of the steps from which he could keep a look-out. Dusky said nothing, but knew well enough what was in his mind.

The day faded under a canopy of crimson glory; night fell, and still there was no sign of the explorers. Their failure to return put Algy in a quandary. He had been asked to remain on the plateau to look after the machine, and he was aware of the danger of leaving his post without letting the others know; all the same, he could not dispel the feeling that something had gone wrong. Ought he to go down Jacob's Ladder and investigate? There seemed to be little point in remaining where he was, for it was hard to see what could happen to the machine, which was still standing, an incongruous object, near the ruins. Again, he reasoned, if he met Biggles and Ginger coming up the path he could always come back with them. In the end he decided that if they had not returned by the time the moon rose he would go in search of them.

He was in some doubt what to do about Dusky, but thought it would be better if he remained behind; the old man, however, when the project was broached, had his

65

own opinion on this, and declared that nothing would induce him to remain in a place which, without any doubt, was haunted by the ghosts of the past.

To this Algy had to submit, and as the silver moon crept up over the distant horizon he set off down the staircase, carrying his rifle, with Dusky following close behind.

By daylight the others had found it a difficult and dangerous journey, but in the uncertain moonlight Algy found the descent an unnerving ordeal. However, he did not hurry, but adopting the principle of slow but sure, moved cautiously down the cornice, hardly looking at the terrible void that fell away on his left. He still hoped to meet the others coming up, but there was no sign of life; no sound broke the heavy silence. He and Dusky might have been the only people on earth.

It was Dusky who, in the first light of the false dawn, spotted the cairn that marked the message which Biggles had left against just such an emergency. Algy picked up the paper, read it, and made Dusky acquainted with its contents.

"They may be all right, but it's strange they should stay away so long," he said. "The only thing we can do is go on to the valley and try to locate them."

They had no difficulty in finding it, and making their way down the rocks, paused to consider the situation, for there was no indication as to which direction they should take; to march straight into the village struck Algy as being a dangerous undertaking, one that might do more harm than good.

Then, as they stood there, in the pitch blackness that precedes the true dawn, they became aware of a curious, not to say alarming, sound. It was a low snarling, punctuated from time to time by a crash, as if a heavy body was being flung against an obstruction. Having listened for a while, Algy asked Dusky what he thought it could be.

The old man answered at once that the snarling could only be caused by a wild beast. He thought it was in a cage, trying to free itself, and he offered to confirm this. Algy assenting to the proposal, he crept away into the darkness.

Not for a moment did it occur to Algy that the sound had any direct connection with Biggles and Ginger. There was no reason why it should. He had no objection to Dusky going off scouting, although for his part he preferred to remain where he was until it became light enough for him to get a better idea of his surroundings.

Pink dawn was beginning to flush the eastern sky when Dusky returned. He said no word, but beckoned urgently. Algy knew that the old man had discovered something, and without a question followed him. Descending to the foot of the rocks, they went on for some distance, keeping clear of the village, and after a while it became obvious that Dusky was making his way towards some outbuildings. As they drew nearer the snarling became louder, and it was clear that the beast, whatever it was, was in one of them. Then, in an interval of silence, came a low mutter of voices, and Algy thought he recognised Ginger's. He now took the lead, and went forward quickly.

Ten yards from the nearest building he stopped, listened for a moment, and then called sharply, "Biggles—is that you?"

The answer came instantly. "Yes, we're in here."

Algy went forward again, and after a minute or two grasped the situation. He found that the building was, in fact, a cage divided into two compartments. In one of them was a black panther. As he came up it was tearing with its claws at the far side of its cage, but as soon as it saw him it turned its attention to him with a rush that made him take a quick pace backwards. However, when he saw that the bars held firmly he moved nearer, and dimly, for it was not yet properly light, made out Biggles and Ginger in the background. Without waiting for explanations he cocked the rifle and took aim at the beast.

Biggles uttered a sharp cry. "Don't shoot!"

"Why not?" demanded Algy, lowering the weapon.

"The shot will bring a crowd here," Biggles told him tersely. "Try to find a way of getting us out. It doesn't matter about the animal."

Algy soon saw the wisdom of this, but a quick reconnaissance revealed that escape was not going to be easy. There was a door to the compartment in which the others were confined, but it was heavily built, and locked, and without the key he was helpless. He passed this information on to Biggles, and then explored farther. The door of the animal's cage was, he discovered, operated from above, as was also the partition, the raising of which would throw the two compartments into one.

"I'd better shoot the brute," he told Biggles desperately. "I could then lift the dividing bars, and by opening the door of the cage, let you out."

"All right—go ahead," agreed Biggles. "As soon as we're out we'll make a dash for the stairway."

Algy raised his rifle, but before he could fire a cry of alarm from Dusky brought him round facing the village. There was no need to look farther. A dozen men, mostly natives, but with some white men among them, were racing towards the spot. One fired a revolver as he ran.

Seeing that it was now too late to put his plan into operation, Algy's first thought was to take cover and try to hold the crowd at bay. Dusky was already on his way to the rear of the buildings, and he followed him, but even as he ran he got an idea that speeded him on.

"Help me up!" he shouted to Dusky, and using the old man's back as a vaulting horse, he scrambled on the roof of the building. Shouts from the oncoming crowd told him that he had been seen, but he gave no heed. Dropping the rifle, he seized the lever which operated the door of the animal's cage, and dragged it back. The door swung open. The panther was not slow to take advantage of the opportunity to escape, and shot out into the open, a streak of black, snarling fury. For a moment it crouched, as if uncertain which way to go; then it saw the crowd, which had stopped at its appearance, and the matter was no longer in doubt. It hated the men on sight, and went towards them like an arrow. The crowd fled, scattering.

Algy would dearly have loved to watch the rest, but there was no time. He raised the partition, and a moment later had the satisfaction of seeing Biggles and Ginger bolt out through the door by which the panther had vacated its prison.

"The stairway!" shouted Biggles. "Make for the stairway."

Algy snatched up his rifle, dropped to the ground, and

in another second all four were in flight towards the rocks. A volley of shots made them look round, and they were just in time to see the panther fall. It had overtaken one of the white men and pulled him down, but the King of the Forest, with a courage worthy of a better cause, emptied his revolver into the animal's sleek flank.

"Keep going! " shouted Biggles. "If we can reach the stairway we can hold them."

Shouts told them that the Tiger was rallying his men to resume the pursuit, and they waited for no more. A few shots were fired as they scrambled up the rocks, but the shooting was wild and the bullets did no harm.

"Good," panted Biggles as they reached the top. "Take cover, everybody. Algy, lend me that rifle."

Crouching behind a rock, he took quick aim and fired at the Tiger. But the run had unsteadied him, and the shot missed. However, it made their pursuers dive for cover. Not that they remained still. They spread out fanwise, and Biggles knew that no good purpose could be served by remaining where they were.

"We'll go on up and get back to the machine," he decided.

In single file they began the long ascent, Biggles, still carrying the rifle, bringing up the rear. He knew, of course, that they would be followed, and was sorry in a way that it had been necessary to reveal the continuation of the staircase, of which, he felt sure, the Tiger was in ignorance.

For half an hour nothing happened, and they toiled on, naturally finding the ascent more arduous than the descent. Then, round a shoulder of rock far below them, appeared the Tiger and his men, also in single file, for the steps were not wide enough to permit the passage of two people abreast. Biggles knew that they, too, must have been seen. He did not shoot, for the range was considerable, and the mounting sun was already causing the air to quiver, making acurate shooting impossible. However, he kept an eye on their pursuers, and presently saw five men, natives, forge rapidly ahead.

"The Tiger has sent some Indians forward," he told the others. "They may be used to this sort of thing, and no doubt the Tiger hopes they'll overtake us. There's nothing to worry about at the moment; if they get too close we'll give them something that should discourage them. Keep going; we're still some way from the top."

For an hour they stuck doggedly to their task, which as time went on, strained their resources to the utmost. The heat became intense, and they were all breathing heavily, although they were still far from the top.

"I think it will pay us to take a breather," announced Biggles presently. "We shall never stand this pace right to the top." He halted at a bend. "This will suit us," he continued, looking back.

Three hundred yards beyond them was another bend, beyond which it was not possible to see.

"The first man who pokes his nose round that corner is going to meet a piece of lead coming the other way," announced Biggles, adjusting his sights, and holding the rifle at the ready.

Squatting on the steps, they recovered their breath. All were thirsty, but there was no water to be had, so no one commented on it. Ten minutes passed, and Biggles was just standing up preparatory to giving the order to march, when, at the lower bend, an Indian appeared. From the abrupt manner in which he stopped it was apparent that he was aware of his danger; but he did not withdraw; he said something to those behind him, the sound being clearly audible in the still air.

Biggles's rifle cracked, and the Indian vacated his position with alacrity, although whether he had been hit or not the comrades could not tell.

"That'll give them something to think about, anyway," observed Biggles, giving the order to march.

Twice during the next hour he halted and surveyed the winding track behind them. There were places where it was possible to see for a considerable distance, but there was no sign of the Indians.

"I don't understand it," he muttered, frowning. "I can hardly think that they've gone back. However, as long as they don't interfere with us I don't care what they do."

They went on, and shortly before midday reached the top of the steps.

"The machine is still all right, anyway," remarked Ginger, noting that it was standing as they had left it.

"We'll go across and have something to eat," declared Biggles.

Hardly had the words left his lips when a rifle cracked, surprisingly close, and a bullet whistled over his shoulder to smack against the rock behind him. So astonished was he that he looked around in amazement, trying to make out the direction from which the shot had come, but there was nothing to indicate it. As, realising his danger, he dashed for cover, there came another shot.

"Where are they coming from?" exclaimed Algy, in tones of surprise and alarm.

"I don't know, but I suspect those Indians know more about this place than we do," answered Biggles, peering cautiously at the surrounding rocks. "Somehow they must have got level with us by another route. If we aren't careful they may outflank us. I think we'd better make a dash for the machine and find a healthier parking place."

"You mean—take off?" queried Ginger.

"Yes."

"Where are you going to make for?"

"The river—there's nowhere else we can go. Besides, we don't want to get too far away. We'll find a quiet anchorage and think things over. When I give the word, run flat out for the machine. We'll open out a bit, so as not to offer a compact target. Ready? Go!"

Jumping up, they all ran towards the machine, but the moment they left cover several shots were fired, which revealed that more than one rifle was being used. However, none of the shots came very close, which struck Biggles as odd until he saw a piece of fabric ripped off the hull of the aircraft.

"They're shooting at the machine!" he shouted. "The rest of you get in and start up, while I hold them off."

They were now within a score of paces of the *Wanderer*. Choosing a shallow depression, Biggles threw himself into it and opened a brisk fire on the spot from where the shots were coming. Puffs of smoke gave the enemies' position away, and he saw that in some way the Indians had reached the high rocks beyond the village, where they had taken cover. He emptied the magazine of his rifle and then dashed to the machine, the engines of which had now been started. As he jumped into the cabin there was a cry of dismay from Ginger.

"They've got the tank!" he shouted. "The petrol is pouring out."

Glancing at the main tank, Biggles saw that this was indeed the case. A lucky shot had struck the tank a glancing blow low down, making a jagged hole, through which petrol was pouring at a rate that must empty the tank in a few minutes. The danger was instantly apparent, for without petrol they would be stranded; the aircraft would be useless, and their only means of getting away would be on foot, down the stairway.

For a moment Biggles tried to plug the hole with his handkerchief; but the spirit still trickled through, and he knew that it could only delay the inevitable end. To make matters worse, shots were still striking the machine, and it could only be a matter of seconds before one of them was hit. He dashed to the cockpit. They had, he saw, just a chance of getting away. If he could only get the machine off the ground, and over the rim of the plateau before the tank emptied itself, they might be able to glide to the river even though the engines were dead.

Algy saw Biggles coming, and guessing what he had in mind, vacated the seat. Biggles flung himself into it, and with a sweep of his hand knocked the throttle wide open. The engines roared. The machine began to move forward. He held the joystick and waited, knowing that it was going to be a matter of seconds. If the engines would continue running for another half minute all might yet be well. If they failed—well, it was better not to think of that.

The machine, now with its tail up, raced on towards the rim of the plateau. Biggles eased the stick back gently, and it lifted. One engine missed fire, roared again, and then, just as the aircraft soared out over the blue forest far below, both died away altogether. The propellers stopped. An uncanny silence fell. But the machine was in the air, gliding towards the nearest loop of the distant river.

New Perils

Had Biggles been asked if he thought the machine, now without motive power, would reach the river, and had he answered truthfully, he would have said "no"; but he knew that it would be a near thing. He had about five thousand feet of height, and some five miles to go, which would normally be within the gliding range of a modern aeroplane. But the *Wanderer* was heavily loaded, and that made a lot of difference. Again, it was not gliding towards an aerodrome where he could be sure of a landing-ground free from obstructions. That part of the river towards which he was gliding—and this, of course, was the nearest part—was new to him, and even if he reached it, there was always a possibility of it turning out to be a death-trap, by reason of dead trees floating on the surface, or sandbanks, or even the giant water-lilies that flourished in many places. However, he had not alternative but to go on, hoping for the best.

The others were well aware of the gravity of the situation, but since they could do nothing about it either, they sat still, watching the grey ribbon of water grow ever more distinct.

Some minutes passed, the aircraft gliding sluggishly at little more than stalling speed. The altimeter now registered two thousand feet, and the river was still a good two miles away.

"You ought to just about do it," Algy told Biggles calmly.

"Just about," answered Biggles, smiling faintly.

The machine glided on, the air moaning softly over its wings. Nobody moved. Nobody spoke.

Ginger watched the river with a sort of helpless fascination. It seemed to float towards them, a narrow lane bordered by a spreading ocean of tree-tops. It was clear that the final issue would be a matter of inches.

Algy afterwards swore that he heard the topmost branches of the trees scrape against the keel as the aircraft just crept over them, to glide down on the water; but that was probably an exaggeration. Ginger sagged a little lower in his seat with relief as the immediate danger passed; provided that there were no obstacles floating on the river all would now be well. Actually there were obstructions, as Biggles afterwards found out, but partly by luck, and partly by skilful flying, he avoided them, and the *Wanderer* sent swarms of crocodiles scurrying as it surged to a standstill on a long, open reach.

Biggles sat back. "Well, so far so good," he announced. "It's time we had a bite to eat. Ginger, get some grub out of the box."

"Wouldn't it be better to make her fast to the bank first?" suggested Algy.

"It probably would—but how are we going to get to the bank?" returned Biggles.

Algy frowned as he realised the significance of Biggles's question. With the engine out of action they were as helpless as if they had been afloat on a raft without a paddle.

"I don't think we need worry about that," resumed Biggles. "We shall drift ashore presently, probably at a bend. As a matter of fact, it suits us to drift downstream, because sooner or later we ought to meet the petrol canoes coming up, and until we repair the tank, and get some juice into it, we're helpless."

"And then what are you going to do?" inquired Ginger.

Biggles shrugged his shoulders. "I don't know," he confessed. "It's a grim business, but we have at least discovered the Tiger's headquarters, and that's something.

I feel inclined to go down to the coast and tell Carruthers about it, and leave it to him to decide on our next move. However, we'll go into that when we've had something to eat."

Squatting on boxes in the little cabin, they made a substantial meal, leaving the *Wanderer* to choose its own course, and in this way perhaps half an hour passed.

It was Dusky who, not without alarm, suddenly called attention to the increased speed of the machine, which could be judged by the rate at which the forest trees on either side were gliding past. At Dusky's shout, the comrades broke off their conversation and climbed out on the hull.

One glance at the river ahead was enough to warn them of their peril, and Biggles could have kicked himself for not taking the possibility into account. Perhaps a quarter of a mile downstream the river plunged between two rocky hills; they were not very high, but they were quite sufficient to force the water into a torrent that boiled and foamed as it flung itself against boulders that had fallen from either side. Already the *Wanderer* was prancing like a nervous horse as it felt the surge of the current, turning slowly, sometimes floating broadside on in the middle of the river. Biggles looked swiftly at either bank in turn, but the nearest was a good fifty yards away, and this might as well have been a mile for all the hope there was of reaching it.

"If she hits one of those rocks she'll crumple like an eggshell!" shouted Algy, steadying himself as the machine gathered speed.

"I suppose it's no use trying to hook the bottom with an anchor?" suggested Ginger.

"No use at all," answered Biggles promptly. "Nothing will hold her now. Grab a spare spar, both of you, and try to fend her off when we come to the rocks. It's our only chance—but for heaven's sake don't fall overboard."

So saying, he snatched up a spare strut and crawled forward until he was lying spreadeagled across the bows. His expression was hard as he looked at the rapids ahead, for there did not appear to be the slightest chance of the *Wanderer* surviving the ordeal that was now inevitable—at any rate, not unless the nose of the machine could he kept straight.

None of them could really say exactly what happened during the next ten minutes. The period was just a confused memory of foaming water and blinding spray. The *Wanderer* bucked and jumped like a live creature, yet somehow, between them, they managed to keep her fairly straight. The greatest mystery was that none of them fell overboard as they thrust with desperate energy at the rocks which seemed to leap up in their path. Then, suddenly, it was all over, and the machine floated smoothly on another stretch of tranquil water.

Biggles crawled back from his hazardous position on the bows, wringing the water from his hair and inspecting the palms of his hands, which had been blistered by the strut. The others were in much the same state, and they sank wearily down to recover their breath and their composure.

"In future we'd better keep an eye on where we're going," muttered Ginger bitterly, gazing ahead as they rounded a bend. His expression became fixed as he stared. Then, with a hoarse cry, he struggled to his feet. "Look out, there's another lot ahead!" he yelled.

Biggles took one look in the direction in which Ginger was staring. Then he snatched up the end of the mooring-rope and dived overboard. Holding the line in his teeth, he struck out for the bank.

Had he not struck shallow water so that he could get his feet on the bottom sooner than he expected, it is unlikely that he would have reached it, for the *Wanderer* was already gathering speed as the river swept on towards the next lot of rapids. But having got his feet planted firmly on a shelving sandbank, he flung his full weight on the rope, and so caused the lightly floating aircraft to swing round near the bank lower down, close enough for Algy and Ginger to seize branches of over-hanging trees, and hang on until the machine could be brought to a safe mooring.

"Who suggested this crazy picnic?" muttered Biggles sarcastically, as, dripping, he climbed aboard.

"I did," grinned Ginger.

"Then perhaps you'll think of a way out of the mess we're in," returned Biggles. "There are rapids below us and rapids above us and our tank is dry. We look like staying here for some time. You might get the tank mended for a start—in case we need it again."

"Okay," agreed Ginger, and went to work. "What are you going to do?" he inquired.

"Walk down the bank to the next lot of rapids, to see how bad they are," answered Biggles. "We've got to make contact with the petrol which Carruthers promised to send before we can do anything. Come on, Algy. You'd better come too, Dusky, in case we need your advice."

Leaving Ginger alone, the others made their way, not without difficulty, down the river-bank, disturbing more than one alligator that lay basking in the stagnant heat. Presently it was possible to ascertain that the rapids stretched for nearly half a mile; they were worse than the first, and Biggles at once dismissed all idea of attempting to shoot them in the aircraft. Beyond the rapids the river resumed its even course, winding placidly through the tropical vegetation. They followed it for some time, but as there appeared to be no change, they were about to start on the return journey when Dusky halted, sniffing like a dog.

"What is it?" asked Biggles quickly.

Dusky's big, child-like eyes opened wide as he whispered nervously that he could smell fire.

Biggles could not understand how this could be, for it seemed impossible that the green jungle, damp in the steaming heat, could take fire; but he followed Dusky, who was now creeping forward silently, every muscle tense, peering into the verdure ahead. After a little while he stopped, and, beckoning to the others, pointed.

Biggles, following the outstretched finger, saw that a little way in front, near the river-bank, the undergrowth had been cut and trampled down, obviously by human agency. In the centre of this area a fire still smouldered. Near it was a brown object, which presently he perceived was a human foot protruding from the debris. Flies swarmed in the still air.

77

"I'm afraid that fellow's dead, whoever he is," murmured Algy in a low voice.

"Sure massa, he dead," agreed Dusky.

Biggles went forward, and a moment later stood looking down at the dead body of a native; he wore blue dungaree trousers, and was clearly one of the more or less civilised natives of the coast. Biggles was still staring at the ugly scene, wondering what it portended, when a groan made him start, and a brief search revealed another native near the edge of the water. This one was not dead, but was obviously dying. Biggles knelt beside him and discovered a gunshot wound in his chest.

"Ask him who he is," he told Dusky.

Dusky knelt beside the wounded man and spoke quickly in a language the others did not understand. The stranger answered weakly, and thereafter followed a disjointed conversation which went on for some minutes—in fact, until the wounded man expired.

Dusky stood up and turned a startled face to his companions. "Dese men bring de petrol in one big canoe," he announced. "Dey get as far as dis and make camp; den Bogat's men come and dey all killed."

"But where is the canoe, and the petrol?" asked Biggles in a tense voice.

Dusky pointed to the river, not far from the bank. "De canoe sink dere," he said. "When Bogat's men rush de camp de paddlers try to get away, but bullets hit canoe and it sink."

"When did this happen?"

"Last night, massa."

Biggles turned to Algy and shrugged his shoulders helplessly. "This is bad," he said quietly. "The petrol was our only chance of getting away."

"But how on earth did the Tiger know that petrol was coming up the river?" demanded Algy.

Biggles laughed bitterly. "Have you forgotten Chorro, Carruthers' assistant? He'd know all about it. As soon as Carruthers got back and ordered the petrol to be brought up to us, Chorro would naturally send the Tiger a message by pigeon post."

Algy nodded. "Of course; that explains it; I'd forgotten that skunk Chorro."

"It looks as if we've only one chance," went on Biggles. "If the water isn't deep we might be able to save some of the petrol cans. Some would probably be punctured by bullets, but not all; if we can recover enough juice to get back to the coast, that's all that matters." He turned to Dusky. "How far out was the canoe when it was sunk?"

Dusky picked up a piece of rotten wood and tossed it on the water about twenty yards from the bank.

Biggles started removing his clothes. "I'll take a dive and try to locate it," he said.

Dusky shook his head vigorously. "Not yet," he protested. "Maybe alligator, maybe piranhas."

"Piranhas?" queried Algy.

"Man-eating fish," explained Biggles. "They're not very big, but they're the most voracious creatures in the world. They swim about in shoals. They've been known to make a skeleton of a man in five minutes."

"Charming little creatures," sneered Algy. "What are we going to do about it?"

Biggles thought for a moment. "We can't get the machine down here, so we'd better make a raft, and work from that. We might be able to locate the canoe by dragging the bottom with our anchor. What do you think, Dusky?"

"Yes, make raft," agreed the old man.

"Then let's go back to the machine and get some tools," suggested Biggles. "It shouldn't be a big job."

"Suppose Bogat's crowd is still hanging about?"

"I hadn't overlooked that possibility," replied Biggles. "We shall have to risk it. Come on, let's get back to the machine."

They went back up the stream, and were relieved to find everything as they had left it. Ginger had just finished repairing the tank with a piece of sheet metal. They told him of their discovery and what they proposed to do, and in a few minutes the necessary equipment for making a raft had been brought ashore—as well as weapons.

"I don't like the idea of leaving the machine," muttered Algy.

"Nor do I, but we can't help it," returned Biggles. "If we work fast we ought to get the raft finished by nightfall, ready to start diving operations tomorrow as soon as it gets light. Let's go."

They marched back to the site of the burnt-out camp, and after burying the unfortunate natives, set about collecting timber suitable for their purpose, in which respect they were guided by Dusky, who knew which wood was light and easy to handle. Some, although Ginger could hardly believe this until he had proved it, was so hard that it turned the edge of an axe.

The sun was sinking in the west by the time the task was finished, and a rough but serviceable raft, moored to a tree, floated against the bank, ready for the morning. Biggles decided that it was too late to start diving operations that day, so, picking up the tools, they made their way back towards the *Wanderer*.

They had not gone very far when, with squeals and grunts, a party of small, hairy pigs came tearing madly down the river-bank. Ginger's first impression was that the animals intended to attack them, but the peccaries—for as such Dusky identified them—rushed past with scarcely a glance. Nevertheless, Dusky eyed them apprehensively, and as they disappeared down the river he held up his hand for silence, at the same time adopting a listening attitude.

In the sultry silence Ginger was aware of vague rustlings in the undergrowth around them, and, exploring with his eyes, soon located the cause. Small creatures, the presence of which had been unsuspected, were leaving their nests in the rotting vegetation and climbing rapidly up the trunks of the trees. He saw a white bloated centipede, a foot long, its numerous ribs rippling horribly under its loathsome skin; a tarantula, a hairy spider as big as his hand, went up a nearby tree in a series of rushes, seeming to watch the men suspiciously every time it halted. This sinister activity gave Ginger an unpleasant feeling of alarm, but he said nothing. He was looking at Dusky askance when, from a distance, came a curious sound, a murmur, like the movement of wind-blown leaves in autumn.

Dusky muttered something and hurried forward, and

there was a nervousness in his manner that confirmed
Ginger's sensation of impending danger.

"What is it?" he asked anxiously.

"De ants are coming," answered Dusky.

At the same time he broke into a run, and it was with
relief that Ginger saw the *Wanderer* just ahead of them,
for by this time the clamour around them had increased
alarmingly. Insects and reptiles of many sorts were climbing trees or plunging through the undergrowth; monkeys
howled as they swung themselves from branch to branch;
birds screeched as they flew overhead. It was an unneces-
sary commotion about a few ants—or so it seemed to
Ginger; but then he had not seen the ants.

It was not until they were within fifty yards of the
machine that he saw them, and even then it was a little
while before he realised that the wide black column which
rolled like molten tar towards them just above the place
where the machine was moored was, in fact, a mass of ants.
Some, in the manner of an advance guard, were well out
in front, and he saw that they were fully an inch and a
half long. Nothing stopped the advance of the insects as
they ran forward, surmounting with frantic speed every
obstacle that lay across their path. The noise made by the
main body, the movement of countless millions of tiny legs
over the vegetation, was a harsh, terrifying hiss, that
induced in Ginger a feeling of utter helplessness. This, he
thought, was an enemy against which nothing could avail.

There was a wild rush for the *Wanderer*, and they
reached it perhaps ten yards ahead of the insect army.
Ginger gave an involuntary cry as a stinging pain, like
a red-hot needle, shot into his leg; but he did not stop—
he was much too frightened. He literally fell into the
machine.

Biggles was the last to come aboard. The mooring-rope
was already black with ants, so he cut it, allowing it to
fall into the water. The machine at once began to drift
with the current, so he ran forward, and dropping the
anchor, managed to get it fast in weeds, or mud. At any
rate, further progress was checked, for the current near
the shore was not strong.

Ginger pulled up the leg of his trousers and saw a scarlet patch of inflammation where the ant had bitten him.

"Get some iodine on that," Biggles told him crisply, and he lost no time in complying, for the pain was acute.

Having done so he joined the others on the deck, from where, in silence and in safety, they watched the incredible procession on the bank. Ginger could not have imagined such a spectacle. The ground was black. Every leaf, every twig, was in motion, as if a sticky fluid was flowing over it. It was little wonder that he stared aghast, not knowing what to say.

"I've seen armies of foraging ants before, but never anything like this," remarked Biggles. "They clean up everything as they go. Heaven help the creature, man, beast or insect, that falls in their path."

"How far do they stretch?" asked Ginger, for as yet he could not see the end of the procession.

Biggles asked Dusky, who announced that the column might extend for a mile, perhaps farther. He had seen the same thing many times, and assured them that if the ants were unmolested they would soon pass on.

The comrades sat on the deck and watched until it was dark, but it was some time later before the volume of sound began to diminish. They then retired to the cabin, where Biggles switched on a light and produced some tins of food.

"We may as well eat, and then get some sleep," he suggested. "We've got to make an early start tomorrow."

Ginger went to sleep, to dream of ants. The forest had taken on a new horror.

Swift Developments

GINGER WAS AWAKENED in the morning by a wild shout from Biggles, a shout that brought him, still half dazed with sleep, to the deck. It was just beginning to get light, and it did not take him long to see what was amiss. The water, which normally was black, was now streaked with yellow, and was swirling past at a speed sufficient to cause the *Wanderer* to drag her anchor. There was, as far as he could see, no reason for this, and he said so.

"It must be raining higher up the river," declared Biggles. "The water is rising fast. We shall have to tie up to the bank—the anchor won't hold."

By this time they were all on deck, and between them the machine was soon made fast to a tree-stump. Biggles stared for a minute at the sky, and then at the river.

"We've no time to lose if we're going to get that petrol," he said urgently. "Apart from the current, with all this mud coming down we soon shan't be able to see a thing under the water. Algy, you stay here and look after things. Ginger, Dusky come with me." So saying, Biggles picked up a length of line, jumped ashore, and set off down the river-bank at a run, Ginger and Dusky following behind. Ginger noted that there was little, if anything, to mark the passage of the ants.

It did not take them long to reach the raft, where the

water was only just becoming discoloured. Biggles carried a large piece of loose rock on board, and pushed off; then, using the rock as an anchor, he brought the raft to a stop over the spot where the canoe had sunk—or as near to it as he could judge. Throwing off his jacket, and holding a spare piece of line, he prepared to dive.

"Here! What about the alligators?" cried Ginger in alarm.

"I shall have to risk it," answered Biggles curtly. "We've got to get some petrol, or we're sunk. Dusky, you keep your eyes open for danger." With this Biggles disappeared under the water.

He had to make three dives before he located the sunken canoe. After this there was a short delay while the raft was moored directly over it. Then the work was fairly straightforward, and had it not been for the rising water, and the discoloration, it would probably have been possible to salve every petrol-can, for Biggles had only to tie the line to a handle while the others hauled it up. As it was, by the time seven cans had been recovered the river was in full spate, and the raft straining at its moorings in a manner which told them that their position was already perilous. With some difficulty they got the raft, with its precious load, to the bank, after which began the work of transporting the cans to the aircraft. By the time this was done the river was a swirling flood, bringing down with it debris of all sorts.

"It's getting worse," announced Algy, with a worried frown, as they poured the petrol into the tank. "We shall never hold the machine here in this, and if she gets into the rapids she's a gonner."

"We'll go down the river to the coast and report to Carruthers," declared Biggles. "It's no use going on with our job while that rat Chorro is at large, advising the Tiger of all our movements. We've got just about enough petrol to do it. Get those empty cans ashore, and stand by to cast off." So saying, Biggles went through to the cockpit.

Algy went forward to cast off the mooring-rope, but seeing that he was having difficulty with it, for the *Wanderer* was pulling hard, Ginger went to his help. At the same time Dusky started throwing the empty cans on the bank. In view of what happened, these details are important. Actually, just what did happen, or how it happened, none of them knew—beyond the fact that the line suddenly snapped. Ginger made a despairing grab at it, slipped, clutched at Algy, and dragged him overboard with him. The Wanderer, breaking free, bucked, and Dusky, caught in the act of throwing, also went overboard. All three managed to reach the bank, while the *Wanderer* went careering downstream. From the bank, Algy, Ginger and Dusky stared at it with horror-stricken eyes, too stunned to speak, helpless to do anything.

Ginger felt certain that the machine would be wrecked in the rapids. Not for a moment did he doubt it. And it was not until he heard the *Wanderer's* engines come to life that he realised that Biggles still had a chance. He could no longer see the machine, for overhanging trees, and a bend in the river, hid it from view. But when, presently, the aircraft appeared in the air above them, and he knew that Biggles had succeeded in getting off, he sat down limply, weak from shock.

Algy looked at the machine, and then at the river.

"He'll never dare to land again," he announced.

"He'd be a fool to try," declared Ginger. "At least, not until the flood had subsided," he added.

They watched the *Wanderer* circle twice; then, as it passed low over them, something white fluttered down, and they made haste to collect it. It was an empty tin; in it was a slip of paper on which Biggles had written, "Wait. Going to coast."

"That's the wisest thing he could do—go down and fill the tank, and let Carruthers know about Chorro," remarked Ginger. "We shan't take any harm here for a few hours."

"I hope you realise that we've no food, and that we haven't a weapon between us except Dusky's knife," muttered Algy.

"In that case we shall have to manage without," returned Ginger.

"Food—me find," put in Dusky confidently, indicating the forest with a sweep of his arm.

"You mean you can find food in the forest?" asked Algy hopefully.

"Sure, boss, I find."

"What sort of food?"

"Honey—roots—fruit, maybe."

"Good. In that case we might as well start looking for lunch."

"You stay—I find," answered Dusky. "Plenty fever in forest. I go now."

"All right, if that's how you want it," agreed Algy.

Dusky disappeared into the gloomy aisles of the jungle.

For some time Algy and Ginger sat on a log gazing moodily at the broad surface of the river. There was little else they could do, for they dare not risk leaving the spot, in case Dusky should return and wonder what had become of them. It did not occur to either of them that they were in any danger. Perhaps they felt that in such a case Dusky would have warned them, although later they agreed that they were both to blame for what happened—but then it was too late.

They did not even see where the natives came from. There was a sudden rush, and before they realised what was happening they were both on their backs, held down by a score or more of savage-looking Indians armed with spears and clubs, bows and arrows. It all happened in a moment of time. Still dazed by the suddenness of the attack they were dragged to their feet and marched away into the forest, menaced fiercely by the spears of their captors. They could do nothing but submit.

In this manner they covered some five miles, as near as they could judge, straight into the heart of the forest before the party halted in an open space on the bank of a narrow stream on which several canoes floated. A few primitive huts comprised the native village. Into one of these they were thrown, and a sentry was placed on guard at the entrance.

Inside, the light was so dim that they could see nothing distinctly, and Ginger was about to throw himself down to rest, for the long march through the oven-like atmosphere had reduced him to a state of exhaustion, when, to his utter amazement, a voice addressed him in English.

"Say, who are you?" inquired the voice, with a strong American drawl.

"Who on earth are *you*?" gasped Ginger when he had recovered sufficiently from his surprise to speak.

"Eddie Rockwell's the name," came the reply.

"What the dickens are you doing here?" demanded Algy.

"Guess that's what I should ask you."

Algy thought for a moment or two. "We're explorers," he announced, somewhat vaguely. "We've got a plane, but our chief has gone to the coast for petrol. While he was away this mob set on us and brought us here. That's all. What about you?"

"My tale is as near yours as makes no difference," answered Eddie quietly.

As their eyes became accustomed to the gloom the comrades saw that he was a young man in the early twenties, but in a sad state of emaciation. His clothes were filthy, and hung on him in rags.

"Having more money than sense, I was fool enough to allow myself to be persuaded to start on a treasure-hunt," continued Eddie. "My father told me that the whole thing was a racket, and I reckon he was about right—but of course I wouldn't believe it."

"A treasure-hunt?" queried Ginger.

"I saw an advertisement in a paper that a couple of guys knew where a treasure was waiting to be picked up. The map they had looked genuine enough, and I fell for it. I financed the expedition, and everything was swell until we got here. Then my two crooked partners just beat it with the stores and left me stranded. If you've tried getting about in this cursed jungle, you'll know what I was up against. However, I did what I could. I blundered about till I struck a stream, and then started down it, figuring that sooner or later, if I could hold out, I'd come to the sea. Instead, I bumped into a bunch of Indians and they brought me here. I didn't care much, because I was pretty well all in. I'd been staggering about without grub for a fortnight, and the Indians did at least give me something to eat. They brought me here, and here I've been ever since. That's all there is to it."

An idea struck Ginger. He realised that these must be the three Americans about whom Carruthers was so concerned. "You've been here for some time, haven't you?" he asked.

"Sure."

"How long?"

"Say, ask me something easier. Weeks, mebbe months."

"These partners of yours," resumed Ginger. "Was one of them a tall, thin, jaundiced-looking bloke, with pale grey eyes and a big mouth, and the other a weedy-looking rat with hay-coloured hair and a wisp of moustache, stained with nicotine?"

Eddie uttered an exclamation of surprise. "Say, that's them," he answered quickly. "I reckon you must have seen them?"

"You bet we have," said Ginger bitterly, and then told their own story with more detail, including the events which had brought them into contact with the two white men in Tiger's secret village. He also mentioned that the disappearance of the party had caused the authorities some trouble.

"Say, now, what d'you know about that!" exclaimed Eddie when he had finished. "Joe Warner and Silas Schmitt —they were my two precious partners—told me that there was a guy hereabouts who was boss of the whole works, but I didn't realise that he was such a big noise as you make out."

"Your partners did, evidently," put in Algy. "They must have known that it was impossible for you to operate here without barging into him or his crowd, so it looks to me as if, having got you to finance them to the spot, they changed sides and left you in the lurch, knowing that you would never be able to get to the coast."

"That's how it looks to me," agreed Eddie. "Can you talk the lingo these natives use?"

"Not a word."

"What do you reckon they'll do with us?"

Algy shook his head. "I've no idea, but judging from their behaviour so far it won't be anything pleasant."

"Then you reckon we haven't a chance of getting away?"

88

"I wouldn't say that. Our chief is down the river, but he'll come back. Moreover, we've got a native servant about somewhere. It just happened that he was out of camp when the attack occurred, but when he gets back he'll guess what has happened, and he ought to be able to trail us. So, on the whole, things may not be as bad as they look."

Eddie seemed to take encouragement from Algy's optimism. The conversation lapsed, Algy peering through one of the many flaws in the side of the hut in an endeavour to see what was going on outside. It seemed that the natives who had captured them were celebrating the event, with considerable noise.

He was still watching when, without warning, a volley of shots rang out from the edge of the jungle. Several Indians fell. More shots followed. There were wild shouts, and the assembled Indians broke up in disorder, scattering and flying for their lives, some into the forest, others flinging themselves into their canoes and paddling away in a panic. Among these was the native who had been on duty at the door of the hut, so there was nothing to prevent those inside from leaving.

For a few seconds Algy hoped that the attack might have been launched by Biggles, who in some miraculous way had returned with assistance; but when Bogat appeared, a rifle under his arm, followed by his gang, his heart, and his hopes, sank.

Bogat saw the three white men at once, and his lips parted in a villainous leer. He covered them with his rifle, and in another moment they were surrounded.

"It looks as if we've fallen out of the frying-pan into the fire," murmured Ginger despondently.

"Who is this guy?" asked Eddie.

Briefly, Ginger told him. There was no time to go into details, for a rope was produced; the prisoners' hands were tied behind them, and a rope was passed from one to the other. Their captors, after setting fire to the huts, formed up in a rough column. Bogat took his place at the head of it, and the party moved off into the forest.

"Where do you suppose they're taking us?" asked Eddie.

"I should say we're on our way to see the King of the Forest," returned Ginger.

A burly half-caste flourished a whip, and put an end to further conversation.

The prisoners trudged on in silence through the green jungle.

The Snake

A

S IT TRANSPIRED, Biggles had just enough petrol to reach the coast. He at once sought Carruthers, who was not a little surprised to see him, and made him acquainted with all that had happened. Carruthers was furious when he heard of the fate of the emergency petrol canoe; but when the real character of Chorro was revealed he was aghast, for he had always regarded him as a trustworthy servant. Unfortunately, nothing could be done about him at the moment, for by a coincidence Chorro had just applied for, and had been granted, three weeks' leave of absence.

"Where's he gone?" inquired Biggles.

"Up the river," answered Carruthers frankly. "He is supposed to have a bungalow somewhere, a matter of two or three days' journey. He's been up the river before."

Biggles smiled grimly. "It's more likely that he's making a visit to the Tiger, to report on the situation."

Carruthers nodded. "I'm afraid you're right," he replied slowly. "Never mind; I'll deal with the scoundrel when he comes back."

"If he does come back," put in Biggles smoothly.

Carruthers gave him an odd look, but made no further comment on the subject. Instead, he asked Biggles what he intended doing.

"Have a bath, a square meal, fill up with petrol and take off again," Biggles told him. "I'm anxious to get back to the others."

"I still don't see how we're going to get hold of the Tiger and his crew," remarked Carruthers, with a worried frown. "I'd come back with you, but at the moment, with the Governor away, I can't leave—at least, not for any length of time."

"I must admit it isn't an easy proposition," acknowledged Biggles. "However, we're getting the hang of things, and sooner or later our chance will come."

Further details were discussed, but nothing definite was arranged, and about two hours later, with full tanks, Biggles set off back up the river, relieved to see that the flood, which apparently had been caused by a local storm, had subsided.

He experienced a pang of uneasiness as he circled low over the camp and saw no sign of the others; but when he landed, taxied up to the bank and jumped ashore, still without them putting in an appearance, his uneasiness turned to alarm. For a few minutes he stood still, occasionally calling, but when this produced no result he began to examine the ground more closely.

Actually there was nothing to show what had happened —not until, in the long grass, he found a broken arrow. Even then he hoped that the arrow might be an old one that had lain there for a long time; but when he looked at the fracture, and saw that it was recent, he knew it was no use deceiving himself. Indians had been to the camp; this was so obvious that he no longer marvelled at the absence of Algy and Ginger. He spent some time hunting about in the bushes, dreading what he might find, and breathed a sigh of relief when his fears proved groundless. "They're prisoners," he told himself, and that was bad enough.

For once he was at a loss to know what to do for the best. He dismissed all thought of the Tiger. He was concerned only with Algy and Ginger, and, to a less extent, Dusky, whom he had left with them. Naturally, they would have to be rescued, but how he was to set about this in the jungle he could not imagine. No project that he could remember had seemed so hopeless.

Not for a moment did he relax his vigilance, for he realised that what had happened to the others might also happen to him. He lit a cigarette and tried to reconstruct the scene, and in so doing came up on the trail leading into the forest. This was a clue which he had not expected, for knowing that the Indians did most of their travelling by canoe, he had assumed that the attack had come from the river.

Now that he had something tangible to go on, he returned to the *Wanderer*, moored the aircraft securely to the bank and made it less conspicuous by throwing reeds and palm fronds over the wings. This done, he went to the cabin, selected a heavy Express rifle from the armoury, filled a cartridge-belt with ammunition and the pockets of his jacket with biscuits. Then, after a final glance round, he set off along the trail, which could be followed without difficulty.

He had not gone far when he was brought to an abrupt halt by a hoarsely whispered "Massa." He recognised the voice at once, but even so, his nerves tingled with shock.

"Dusky!" he called tersely. "Where are you?"

Dusky dropped out of a tree and hurried to him.

"What happened?" asked Biggles shortly, wondering how the old man had escaped.

This Dusky soon explained. In mournful tones he related how he had gone into the forest to find food, a quest which—fortunately for him, as it happened—had taken him into a tree. The tree was at no great distance from the camp, and the sound of the assault had reached his ears. From his hiding-place he had watched Algy and Ginger being led away into the jungle. He apologised for not going to their rescue, but pointed out that, as the only weapon he had was a knife, he was in no position to take on a crowd of Indians. This Biggles did not dispute. Indeed, when Dusky explained that he had remained 'n hiding, waiting for him to come back so that he could tell him what had happened, he congratulated him on his common sense.

"I suppose you've no idea where the Indians have gone?" asked Biggles.

Dusky shook his head, saying that he did not know the district, but gave it as a matter of opinion that the Indian village would not be far away.

"In that case we shall have to try to find it," Biggles told him.

Dusky agreed, but without enthusiasm.

They continued on down the trail, Dusky now leading the way and stopping from time to time to listen. This went on for an hour, by which time, although they did not know it, they were getting near the village.

The first intimation of this came when shouts and yells reached their ears, sounds which Dusky interpreted correctly, as the Indian way of making jubilation over the capture of the white men.

They now proceeded with more caution, and were peering forward through the undergrowth hoping to catch sight of the village when a volley of shots sent them diving for cover. The shots, however, did not come their way, which puzzled Biggles more than a little. Dusky went up a tree like a squirrel, to return in a few moments with the unwelcome news that Bogat and his gang had attacked the Indians, scattered them, and taken over their prisoners. He also announced that there was another white man with Algy and Ginger.

Biggles wasted no time in futile guessing as to who this could be. He was too concerned about Algy and Ginger. He thought swiftly, undecided how to act.

"How many men has Bogat got with him?" he asked Dusky.

Dusky opened and closed his hands, twice.

"Twenty, eh?" muttered Biggles.

To attack twenty men single-handed—for Dusky could hardly be counted on—would be, he saw, a rash undertaking. With the advantage of surprise in his favour he might shoot two or three of them, but in the ensuing battle, even if he escaped, Algy and Ginger would be certain to get hurt. He perceived, too, that if he failed in an attempt at rescue now, the odds against him in future would be worse, for once his presence was revealed strict guard would be kept. Taking all the factors into consideration, he decided that it would be better to wait for a more favourable opportunity. Perhaps a chance would come after dark.

At this point Dusky, who had again ascended a tree, returned to say that Bogat and his men, with their prisoners, were moving off through the forest. This at once upset Biggles's plans, for he had assumed that Bogat would remain in the village for a while. To attack him while he was on the march was obviously out of the question, so he took the only course that remained open, which was to allow Bogat's party to go on and follow as close behind as was reasonably safe.

He told Dusky his plan, and the old man agreed, so after waiting for a little while to give Bogat a start, they once more took up the trail.

Biggles of course had not the remotest idea of where they were going, nor even if they were travelling north or south, for the green jungle hemmed them in on both sides, and overhead. Nor, for a long time, did Dusky know; but eventually the trail crossed another which he recognised as one he had used when collecting chicle for the Tiger.

"I reckon Bogat go to de Tiger's village," he announced.

"But that's up in the mountains," Biggles pointed out.

Dusky nodded. "Sure. By-um-by we come to old ruins at bottom of steps. Maybe Bogat stop dere; maybe he go up steps to de king."

"You're sure you know where we are?"

"Yes, I'se sure, massa."

"How far is it from here to the foot of the steps?"

"Half an hour's march—maybe a little more, or less."

"If we're as close as that, then there must be a risk of our running into some of Bogat's Indians, chicle-collectors, or labourers."

"Tha's right, massa."

"In that case we'd better stay here and do a bit of thinking. Let's find a place where we can hide until it gets dark."

Dusky turned aside from the trail and soon found a sheltered retreat.

Here they remained until the light, always dim beneath the towering tree-tops, turned to the gloom of evening. They saw no one, and heard nothing except the natural sounds of the forest. Once, a panther, as black as midnight, slunk past with twitching tail: it saw them, and its baleful yellow eyes glowed, but it made no attempt to attack them, and Biggles was relieved to see it pass on.

Dusky shivered. "Dat's de debbil," he muttered nervously.

"Forget it, Dusky. Devil or no devil, I warrant that he'd find an expanding bullet from this rifle a nasty pill to take."

"He put a spell on you, den you can't shoot."

"He won't put any spell on me, I'll promise you," returned Biggles lightly.

"I reckon you don't believe in spells, massa?"

"No, I don't," answered Biggles shortly.

"Den you watch out dem big snakes dey call anaconda don't get you. Why, everyone knows dey bewitch folks." Dusky shivered again.

"I've heard that tale before, but I should have to see it before I believed it," murmured Biggles cynically.

"Maybe if you stay in de forest long enough, you see," whispered Dusky knowingly.

Biggles did not pursue the subject, and nothing more was said for some time.

"You know, massa," said Dusky after a long silence, "I reckon de gang don't work down here no longer. You remember I said about de gang working at de bottom of de steps?"

"What makes you think they've gone?"

"Cos I don't hear nothing. Dem boys would sure be hollerin'."

"Hollering? Why?"

"When Bogat's men crack dere whips on dere backs."

"I see. How can we make sure? Shall I go and have a scout round?"

"Not you, massa," said Dusky quickly. "I go. I don't make no noise. You stay right here. I find out what's going on."

"You're sure you'll be able to find me again?"

"Sure, massa. Dere's a wide stretch of savannah just ahead—I go dat way."

"All right," Biggles agreed, somewhat reluctantly, and Dusky glided away, to be quickly lost in the shadows of the primeval forest.

96

An hour passed, so Biggles judged, and he began to get worried, for it was now quite dark, and he was by no means certain—in spite of Dusky's assurance—that the old man would be able to find him again.

As time went on and there was still no sign of him, Biggles became definitely concerned. He stood up and whistled softly, but there was no reply. Something—he could see what—slithered away in the undergrowth.

Staring in the direction which Dusky had taken Biggles became aware of an eerie blue glow, but taking a few paces forward, he soon solved the mystery. It was moonlight shimmering on a thin mist that had formed in an open glade, evidently the savannah to which Dusky had referred. He was about to turn back to the rendezvous, for he had no intention of leaving it, when a movement on the edge of the blue light caught his eye. It was, he saw from the shape of the object, a human being. Moving quickly but quietly to the edge of the clearing, he saw, as he hoped, that it was Dusky; but what the old man was doing he could not imagine. His movements were peculiar. With his arms held out in front of him, and his head thrown back, he was walking slowly across the savannah, step by step, towards the middle of it, in the uncertain manner of a person walking in his sleep.

As Biggles watched this strange scene he became aware of a queer musty smell that reminded him vaguely of something, but he could not remember what it was. At the same time he was assailed by a sensation of impending danger far stronger than anything he had ever before experienced. It was so acute that he could feel his nerves tingle, and presently beads of perspiration began to form on his forehead. This was something new to him, but his response was irritation rather than fear—perhaps because he could not see anything to cause alarm. Alert for the first sign of danger, walking softly, he moved forward on a line that would intercept Dusky somewhere about the middle of the savannah.

He could still see nothing to account for it, but as he advanced his sensations approached more nearly to real fear than he could ever recall. The only object that he could see, apart from the surrounding vegetation, was what appeared to be a black mound rising above the rough grass, and it was towards this that Dusky was stepping with slow, mechanical strides. A sudden suspicion darted into Biggles's brain, and he increased his pace; and even as he did so the mound moved. Something in the centre of it rose up sinuously, and remained poised. It was the head of a snake, but of such a size that Biggles's jaw dropped in sheer amazement.

For a moment he could only stare, thunderstruck, while the great flat head began to sway, slowly, with hideous grace. Then Biggles understood, and, with knowledge, power returned to his limbs.

"Dusky!" he shouted hoarsely.

But he might have remained silent for all the notice the old man took.

"Dusky!" he shouted again. "Stop!"

The old man continued to walk forward, arms outstretched, as though to embrace a friend.

A cry of horror broke from Biggles's lips, and he dashed forward. At a distance of ten paces from the mound, which he saw was coil after coil of snake, he halted, and raising his rifle, tried to take aim. Perspiration was pouring down his face. The stench was now overpowering. The mist caused the target to dance before his eyes, yet he knew that it would be worse than useless to fire blindly into the body of the creature. It must be the head or nothing.

To make sure, there was only one thing to do, and he did it. He ran in close, took deliberate aim at the squat head now turning towards him, and fired.

In the silent forest the crash of the explosion sounded like the crack of doom. It was followed, first, by a wild scream from Dusky, who fell flat on his face, and, secondly, by a series of furious smashing thuds, as if a tornado was flinging down the mighty trees. The mound was no longer there; instead, the centre of the clearing was occupied by seemingly endless coils which, with insensate fury, threshed and looped over and among the rank glass. The end of one such loop caught Biggles in the back and sent him spinning, but he was up again in an instant; waiting only to recover the rifle, which had been knocked out of his hands, he caught Dusky by the scruff of the neck and dragged him like an empty sack towards the edge of the jungle. Behind him, the crashing and thumping continued with unabated fury, and he recalled vaguely having read somewhere that even if it is decapitated, the anaconda, the great snake of the Central American forests, may take twenty-four hours to die.

Dusky began to howl, so Biggles stopped and dragged him to his feet. "Shut up," he snapped. "You're not hurt."

"Oh, massa, oh, massa, I thought dat ole snake had got me," moaned Dusky.

"Come on, let's get out of this," growled Biggles, who, to his disgust, was more unnerved than he would have cared to admit.

Dusky, with many a nervous backward glance, followed him obediently back to the rendezvous.

"What made you go blundering towards the snake as if you were crazy?" inquired Biggles, half angrily, half curiously.

"I didn't see no snake, massa," answered Dusky weakly.

"Then how did you know it was there?"

"I dunno, massa. I just knew, that's all."

"So you went up to it? What were you going to do —play with it?" sneered Biggles.

"I just couldn't help going," protested Dusky. "De snake called me, and I went. I told you dem ole snakes bewitch folks."

"Well, that one won't do any more bewitching," replied Biggles crisply. He knew it was useless to argue with the old man, for nothing would shake his inherent conviction that he had been bewitched. Indeed, Biggles, to his annoyance, had an uneasy feeling that there might be something in the superstition after all, for he himself had been conscious of a sensation for which he could not account.

He could still hear the dying monster flinging itself about in the savannah, but he knew there was nothing more to be feared from it.

"Come on, Dusky, pull yourself together," he exclaimed. "I've blown the snake's head off, so it can't hurt you now. I only hope that my shot was not heard by Bogat or the Tiger. Are you feeling better?"

"Dusky!" he shouted. *"Stop!"*

Dusky drew a deep breath. "Yes, massa," he said shakily, "I'se better now. But dat ole snake——"

"Forget about it," snapped Biggles.

"Yes, massa."

"Were you on your way back?"

"Yes, massa."

"Then you've been to the bottom of the steps? What did you discover?"

"Just like I said, massa—dey's gone."

"Gone? What do you mean?"

Dusky explained that he had been right up to the foot of the stairway, to the spot where, at the time of his escape, he had been forced to dig with the gang working among the ruins. These diggings were now abandoned except for one old man who had been left in charge of a store-shed. This old fellow was well known to Dusky; he was one of the forced labourers, and consequently had no love for his taskmasters. For this reason Dusky had not hesitated to reveal himself; but except for the fact that everyone, including the newly captured white men, had gone to some distant place far up the stairway to dig in some fresh ruins, he knew nothing.

"If he said distant place, it rather looks as if they've gone right up to the top—to the plateau where we landed the machine," said Biggles thoughtfully. "There are some ruins up there, as we know. Had they only gone to the valley where the king's house is situated, he would have said so."

Dusky agreed.

"Then we shall have to go up there, too," announced Biggles.

"We get captured fo' sure," muttered Dusky dubiously.

"I can't see any alternative," continued Biggles. "We can't just sit here and do nothing—they might be up there for months."

"How about de airplane?" suggested Dusky.

"That's no use. We couldn't land on the plateau without being seen or heard. No, Dusky, I'm afraid it means going up on foot, but you needn't come if you don't want to."

"I don't want to, but I'll come," offered the old man courageously.

Biggles thought for a moment. "I'll tell you what, though. I shall be pretty conspicuous in these clothes. If I could make myself look a bit more like one of the workmen I might be taken for a slave if we are seen. Is there any chance of getting an old pair of blue pantaloons, like those you wear?"

Dusky thought he could get a pair at the store-shed.

"That old man won't betray us, I hope?"

"No, sah," declared Dusky emphatically. "He like the rest, be glad if you killed de Tiger so dey can all go back to de coast. He'll help us. I make your face brown with berries, den you look like a no-good Indian."

Biggles smiled in the darkness. "That's a good idea. Let's start. There will be less chance of our being seen if we travel by night. Can you find your way to the store-shed? I can't see a blessed thing."

"You foller me, massa; I show you," said Dusky simply.

They set off. Dusky was never at fault, but the darkness was such that progress was necessarily slow, and it was some time before they reached the foot of the steps, where, in the store-shed, the old watchman crouched over a smouldering fire. He made no difficulty about finding a pair of ragged pantaloons, and this was the only garment Biggles put on. Really, in the steamy heat of the jungle, he was glad of an excuse to discard his own clothes, which the watchman hid under a pile of stones. Without guessing how much was to depend on them, Biggles transferred his cigarettes and matches to the pocket of his new trousers.

He was in some doubt about the rifle, for it was obvious that he could not carry it without it being seen. In the end he decided to take it, even if it became necessary to hide it somewhere later on. His automatic he strapped to his thigh, under his trousers. Meanwhile, Dusky and the old watchman, taking a torch, had gone into the forest, and presently returned with a load of red berries. These were boiled in an iron pot, and after the liquid had cooled Biggles more or less gave himself a bath in it. Fortunately, he could not see himself, or he might have been alarmed at the change, for instead of being white he was now the colour of coffee.

Thanking the watchman, and promising him deliverance from servitude in the near future, Biggles and Dusky set off on their long climb up Jacob's Ladder.

They came first to the valley in which the village was situated; but all was silent, so they wasted no time there. Continuing on up the steps, they found themselves just below the summit about two hours before dawn—as near as Biggles could judge.

Here he turned off into a narrow ravine, for he was tired to the point of exhaustion. Dusky appeared to suffer no such inconvenience, and offered to keep watch while he, Biggles, had a short sleep, an offer that Biggles accepted, and ordered Dusky to wake him at the first streak of dawn.

He appeared to have done no more than close his eyes when Dusky was shaking him by the shoulder. Before dropping off to sleep he had made his plan, and this he now put into execution.

"You're going to stay here," he told Dusky. "You can take charge of the biscuits and the rifle and wait until I come back. If I'm not back within forty-eight hours you can reckon that I've been caught, in which case try to make your way to the coast and let Mr. Carruthers know what's happened. All being well, I shall be back here, with the others, before very long. Keep under cover."

With this parting injunction, Biggles went back to the steps, and after a cautious reconnaissance moved on towards the top. He now proceeded with the greatest care; and it was as well that he did, for while he was still a hundred feet from the top he was mortified to see a man sitting on a rock, a rifle on his arm, obviously doing duty as sentry. To pass him without being seen was clearly impossible, so Biggles, after exploring the cliff on his left for the best place, scaled it, and went on through a chaos of rocks towards the plateau. Guided now by distant shouts, and the occasional crack of a whip, he worked his way forward, and presently, as he hoped, found himself in a position overlooking the plateau.

To his right, perhaps a hundred yards away, sat the sentry at the head of the stairway. With this man he was not particularly concerned—at any rate, for the time being. Immediately in front, and slightly below, lay the ruined village. Here a gang of men was working with picks and shovels, or carrying away baskets of earth. Altogether, there were about forty workmen, and Biggles had no difficulty in picking out Algy, Ginger, and the stranger. They were working close together. Watching the gang were six guards, standing in pairs. They carried rifles. Another man, an enormous Indian, walked amongst the labourers swishing a vicious-looking whip. Not far away, in the shade of a ruined house, squatted the Tiger and his two white companions. Close behind them stood two natives in tawdry uniforms; they also carried rifles, and were evidently a sort of bodyguard. Beyond, shimmering in the heat of the morning sun, the plateau lay deserted.

For some time Biggles lay still, surveying the scene thoughtfully. A big patch of grotesque prickly pear attracted his attention, and he saw that if he moved along a little to the left he could use this as a screen to cover an advance into the village. Once among the houses, it should, he thought, be possible to get right up to the gang of workmen, and so make contact with Algy and Ginger—which was his main object. Beyond that he had no definite plan.

Like a scouting Indian he backed down from his elevated position and began working his way towards the prickly pear.

Ginger gets Some Shocks

WHEN ALGY, Ginger and Eddie had been marched off through the forest by Bogat they did not know where they were being taken, but, naturally, they could make a good guess. Unless Bogat had some scheme of his own, it seemed probable that they would be taken to the Tiger. This suspicion was practically confirmed when they reached the foot of the stairway. Two hours later, utterly worn out, and in considerable discomfort from insect bites and scratches, they were standing before the King of the Forest, who eyed them with undisguised satisfaction.

In his heart, Ginger expected nothing less than a death sentence, but that was because he did not realise the value of labour in the tropics, particularly white labour, which is always better than native work. It was, therefore, with relief that he received the news that they were to be put in the slave-gang. Algy, being older, perceived that this was, in fact, little better than a death sentence; that without proper food, clothes and medical treatment, they were unlikely to survive long in a climate which sapped the vitality even of the natives. However, he agreed with Ginger's optimistic observation that while they were alive there was hope; for, after all, Biggles was still at large. Whether or not he would ever learn what had happened to them was another matter. They were not to know that Dusky had been a witness of the attack.

They were in evil case by the time they reached the plateau, for they had been given only a little maize bread and water, barely enough to support life. The stench of the stone building, little better than a cattle-pen, into which on arrival they were herded with the other slaves, all Indians or half-castes, nearly made Ginger sick. Life under such conditions would, he thought, soon become intolerable.

Tired as they were, sleep was out of the question, and they squatted miserably in a corner, waiting for daylight. At dawn the door was opened by a man who carried a heavy whip; behind him were six other men carrying rifles. A quantity of food, in the nature of swill, was poured into a trough; upon this the slaves threw themselves like animals, eating ravenously with their hands, scooping up the foul mixture in cupped palms. The three white men took no part in this performance.

A few minutes only were allowed for this meal, after which the gang was formed into line and made to march past a shed from which picks and shovels were issued. Thus equipped, they went to what had once been the main street of the village, where a shallow trench had been opened. The gang-boss cracked his whip and the slaves started work, deepening and extending the trench.

"What do you suppose we're doing?" asked Ginger, getting into the trench behind Algy.

"Probably laying the telephone," returned Algy sarcastically.

"Ha, ha," sneered Ginger. "Very funny."

The gang-boss advanced, brandishing his whip. "No talking," he snarled.

Ginger drove his pick viciously into the sun-baked earth, and thereafter for a while work proceeded in silence.

"Here comes the Tiger," murmured Algy presently.

"I'll tear the stripes off his hide one day," grated Eddie. "They can't do this to me."

"It seems as though they're doing it," grunted Algy.

Ginger went on working. There was no alternative, for he had no wish to feel the whip across his shoulders.

A few minutes later, standing up to wipe the perspiration out of his eyes, he noticed something. It was nothing spectacular. He had already realised, from the nature of the ground, which consisted largely of broken paving-stones, that the trench was crossing the foundations of what must have been a large building. One or two of the supporting columns, although they had been broken off short, were still standing; one such column was only a few paces away on his right, and without any particular interest his eyes came to rest on it. They were at once attracted to a mark—or rather, two marks. At first he gazed at them without conscious thought; then, suddenly, his eyes cleared as he made out that the marks were initials.

There were two sets, one above the other. The lower ones had almost been obliterated by the hand of time, after the manner of an old tombstone, but it was still possible to read the incised scratches. They were the letters E.C., and were followed by the date, 1860. There was no need for him to look closely at the date of the initials above to see that they were comparatively recent. The letters were L.R., and the date 1937. A suspicion, dim as yet, darted into Ginger's mind. He threw a quick glance at the gang-boss to make sure that he was not being watched, and then leaned forward to confirm that his reading of the lower initials had been correct. In doing this he put his hands on the end of a stone slab in such a way that his weight fell on it. Instantly it began to turn as though on a pivot, and he flung himself back with a gasp of fear, for he had a nasty sensation that he had nearly fallen into an old well. Another quick glance revealed the gang-boss walking towards him, so he went to work with a will, aware that he was slightly breathless.

The lash swished through the air, but without actually touching him. It was a warning, and he took it—at least, while the boss was within hearing. Then he spoke to Algy, who was working just in front of him.

"Algy," he whispered, "you remember Biggles talking about a treasure supposed to have been discovered in these parts by a fellow named Carmichael?"

"Yes."

"What was his Christian name, do you remember?"

"No—why?"

"Do you remember the date?"

"Yes—1860."

"Then this is where Carmichael came. I've just seen his mark. Go on working—don't look round."

Ginger now spoke under his arm to Eddie, who was behind him.

"Eddie, you said you come here on a treasure-hunt?"

"Sure I did."

"There was a map, I believe?"

"That's right."

"Who drew it?"

"A guy named Roberts—Len Roberts."

"And was there a date?"

"Sure. It was 1937. What's the idea? Do you reckon we're on a treasure-hunt now?"

"I'm certain of it," replied Ginger. "You see that paper the Tiger is looking at? Does that look like your map?"

"It sure does."

"Then it's the treasure we're after. We're driving a trench right across the area where it is supposed to be."

At this point, much to Ginger's disgust, further conversation was interrupted by an Indian, who dropped into the trench between him and Eddie.

"Here, you, get out of the way," grunted Ginger, hoping that the man would understand what he meant.

"Go on digging," answered a voice quietly.

Ginger started violently, and nearly dropped his pick. His nerves seemed to twitch, for there was no mistaking the voice. It was Biggles.

"Go on digging," said Biggles again. "Don't look round. Tell Algy I'm here."

Ginger, who seemed slightly dazed, passed the incredible information on to Algy, first warning him to be ready for a shock. He then worked in silence for a little while, watching the guards.

Choosing a favourable moment, he snatched a glance behind him under his arm. "How did you get here?" he whispered.

"Never mind that—I'm here," breathed Biggles. "Did I hear you say something about a treasure?"

"Yes, I reckon we're digging for it."

"What makes you think so?"

"Take a look at that column on your right. Carmichael's initials are on it, and the date, 1860. Those above are those of the chap who made the map that brought Eddie here. He's the fellow behind you. Incidentally, he is one of the party of missing Americans Carruthers told us about. His partners abandoned him in the forest—they're the two fellows over there with the Tiger. He was caught by the Indians, and Bogat captured us together. Can you get us out of this jam?"

"That's what I'm here for."

"Then for the love of Mike do something."

"Don't be in a hurry," said Biggles softly, pretending to work. "I'm thinking. You go on as if nothing unusual had happened."

"How did you know we were here?"

"I found Dusky, and he trailed you. He's back in a ravine waiting for us. Don't talk any more now, or that big stiff with the whip may get suspicious."

Nothing more was said. The only sounds were the thud of picks, the scrape of shovels, the grunts of the slaves and the cracking of the whip.

Biggles considered the question of escape from every angle before making up his mind, but in the end he determined to act forthwith. There was no point in delaying the action, for the position was not likely to alter before sunset, and he had no intention, if it could be avoided, of passing the night under lock and key. In any case, he thought there might be an evening roll call, in which case the discovery of an extra man would be inevitable.

He told Algy, Ginger and Eddie to draw closer together so that they could hear what he had to say without making it necessary for him to raise his voice. He still knew practically nothing about Eddie apart from what Ginger had said, but it was obvious that he was a prisoner like the rest, in which case he would be anxious to escape. Apart from that, he would be an extra man on his side.

"Listen," he said. "We shall have to make a dash for it. There's no other way that I can see. We've got two useful factors on our side. The first is surprise—you can see from the way the guards are standing that the last thing they imagine is that they will be attacked. The second

109

factor is my automatic. I'm afraid I shall have to use it. This is no time for niceties. This is what I'm going to do, and what I want you to do."

Here Biggles had to pause and make a pretence of scraping earth from the bottom of the trench while the gang-boss went past. As soon as the man was out of ear-shot he continued:

"The next time those two nearest guards come this way I shall jump out of the trench and cover them with my gun to make them drop their rifles. If they refuse, I shall shoot. Either way, you'll grab the rifles and open fire on the other guards along the line. Don't get flustered. Be sure of hitting your man. In this way we ought to put four of them out of action before the others guess what's happening. If I know anything about it, when we start shooting they'll run."

"What about the Tiger?" asked Ginger.

"Never mind about him for the moment. Having got the weapons, we'll fight a rearguard action to the top of Jacob's Ladder. If we can reach it, the rest should be easy. Is that all clear?"

The others, including Eddie, announced that it was.

"Then stand by," whispered Biggles tersely. "The guards are coming this way. Remember, speed is the thing."

The two guards to whom Biggles had referred, both half-castes, were walking slowly along the line of workmen. Strolling would perhaps be a better word. Hand-made cigarettes hung from their lips. One carried his rifle care-lessly in the crook of his arm; the other held his weapon at the trail; and it was clear from their careless manner that they did not expect trouble. Thus does familiarity breed contempt, and Biggles judged correctly when he guessed that the men had performed their task every day for so long that they no longer apprehended danger. They sauntered along, smoking and chatting, throwing an occasional glance at the labourers. Biggles stooped a little lower in the trench, gripped his automatic firmly, finger on trigger, and waited.

He waited until they drew level. Then with a quick movement he stepped out in front of them, the pistol held low down on his hip.

"Drop those guns," he rasped.

Never was surprise more utter and complete. The behaviour of the guards was almost comical. First they looked at Biggles's face, then at the pistol, then back at his face, while their expressions changed from incredulity to fear. Neither spoke. One of them dropped his rifle; or rather, it seemed to fall from his nerveless hands. The other made a quick movement as though he intended shooting. Biggles did not wait to confirm this. His pistol cracked, and the shot shattered the man's arm. The rifle fell, and he fled, screaming. This, the opening operation, occupied perhaps three seconds, and as it concluded Algy and Ginger played their parts. In a moment they had snatched up the fallen rifles and opened fire on the two guards next along the line. One spun round and fell flat. The other made a leap for the trench, but stumbled and fell before he reached it, the rifle flying from his hand.

"Come on," snapped Biggles, and sprinted towards the spot.

The four white men had almost reached the second pair of rifles before the full realisation of what was happening penetrated into the minds of the other people on the plateau—the Tiger, his two white conspirators, his bodyguard, the two remaining guards, and the slaves. An indescribable babble, like the murmur of a wave breaking on shingle, rose into the still air. Then, abruptly, it was punctuated by shots from several directions. Some of them came near the fugitives, but none of them was hit. Biggles saw a workman drop.

While Eddie picked up the two rifles he looked round and saw that the situation had changed but little. The two remaining guards had run for some distance; then, taking cover, they had started firing. The Tiger was shooting with a revolver and shouting orders at the same time, and the uproar he created was hardly calculated to encourage his bodyguard to take careful aim. They were shooting, but with more speed than accuracy. The two renegade white men were firing their revolvers, but the range was too long for accurate shooting.

"All right," said Biggles crisply. "Let 'em have it."

Four rifles spat in the direction of the Tiger's party.

One of the bodyguard fell; all the rest dived for cover, and disappeared behind the house.

"Start moving towards the stairway," ordered Biggles. "I'll cover you."

He knelt down and opened a steady fire on the building behind which the Tiger and his party had taken refuge, while under his protective fire the others hurried towards Jacob's Ladder.

So far Biggles's plan had worked without a hitch, and it seemed as if the stairway would be reached without difficulty, and without serious danger. But, unfortunately, the man who had been on guard at the head of the steps, and who had disappeared at the first shots, now came back, and kneeling behind a boulder, opened a dangerous fire.

Biggles had assumed, naturally, that the man had bolted, but hearing the shots he looked round quickly and realised what had happened. He did not waste time wondering why the man had returned; he was concerned only with the danger he represented.

Biggles dashed on after the others. "We shall have to work round that chap," he said curtly. "Algy, come with me. We'll go to the left. The others go to the right. We'll get him from the flank."

But before this manœuvre could be made, a new factor arose, one that instantly made Biggles's scheme impracticable. He realised why the guard, who had bolted down the steps, had returned. He had not come back alone. At the top of Jacob's Ladder now appeared Bogat, and behind him nearly a score of armed men. They took in the situation at a glance, and spreading out, taking cover behind rocks, effectually blocked the steps.

Biggles perceived that Bogat and his gang must have been actually coming up the steps all the time. It was unfortunate, but it couldn't be prevented. In any case, he was not to know it. It was one of those unexpected mischances that can upset the best-laid plan. To advance in the face of a score of rifles was obviously a hopeless proposition; nor could they remain where they were. In the circumstances he gave the only reasonable order, which was to retire.

"Get back to the village! " he shouted. "We'll find cover in one of the buildings while we think things over. Keep together. Don't waste ammunition. Run for it."

Dodging among the boulders, for shots were now whistling, they made a quick but orderly retirement to the buildings. It was fortunate that they had not far to go. Biggles selected a group of stone houses near the spot where, a few minutes before, they had been working.

"This will do," he decided, and dived through the doorway to temporary safety. The others followed him.

"Anyone hurt?" he inquired.

Eddie had been slightly wounded in the forearm, that was all; he made light of it, and tore a strip off his shirt for a bandage.

"Sorry, chaps," said Biggles apologetically. "The show came unstuck. Bad luck we chose the moment that Bogat and his toughs were coming up the steps. Not being able to see through solid rock, I wasn't to know that. Still, I think we ought to be able to hold them off this place for some time—at any rate, long enough to enable us to work out a new plan. Keep watch through the windows, but don't show yourselves. Phew! Isn't it hot."

Eddie drew his sleeve across his forehead. "You're telling me."

Strange Events

FOR SOME TIME they kept careful watch, but saw
nothing of the Tiger or his associates. Sounds told
them that the labourers had been herded back into
their pen.

"What's going on, I wonder?" muttered Ginger at last.

Biggles answered. "I should say that the Tiger, knowing
we are on the plateau, has posted a strong guard at the
head of the stairway. We are, he supposes, in a trap, and
he has only to close the mouth of it to keep us in. Why
should he hurry? He knows that we can't stay here
indefinitely without food and water. No doubt he's watching the place from a distance. Then again, he may not be
sure which house we are actually in, and doesn't feel like
taking the risk of being shot in order to find out."

"Did you come up the stairway?" asked Ginger.

"Not exactly," returned Biggles. "I came nearly to the
top, but seeing a fellow on guard, made a detour and
came in over the escarpment behind the village—at the
back of those prickly pears."

"Couldn't we get out that way?"

Biggles thought for a moment. "Possibly. We could, of
course, if no guards were posted, but I can't think that
the Tiger would be such a fool as to shut the front door
and forget to lock the back door—so to speak. The way I
came must have been the way the Indians came when they
chased us up the steps after we had escaped from the black

114

panther. One thing is certain: it would be silly to try to get out of here in broad daylight. We'll wait for dark."

It seemed a long wait—as indeed it was. Silence settled over the plateau. The sun struck down with bars of white heat. The only sound was the languid buzz of insects.

The shadows were lengthening when Ginger suddenly recalled the pivoting flagstone; he could see it from where he stood on guard at a window, not a score of paces away. In the rush of events following Biggles's arrival he had forgotten all about it.

"Here, Biggles," he said, "I've just remembered something." In a few words he told the others of his curious discovery.

"Sounds interesting," was Biggles's comment.

"You mean, the treasure might be in there?" put in Eddie. Biggles had by this time learned who Eddie was, and how he came to be with the party.

"It might be, but, to tell the truth, I wasn't thinking about that," answered Biggles. "It would be useful, of course, to locate the treasure, although I don't think we're in a position to clutter ourselves up with it at the moment. Our job is to get out. What I was thinking was that under Ginger's slab there might be a tunnel leading to another part of the plateau. At any rate, if there is a cave or something there it ought to be worth exploring."

"Now?" queried Ginger.

"No. We'll wait till it gets properly dark."

"There's no need for us all to go," remarked Ginger. "I know just where the thing is. I could explore, and then come back and let you know what's inside—if there is an inside."

"That's a good idea," agreed Biggles. And so it was decided.

Night came. The moon had not yet risen, but the sky was clear, and the stars gave as much light as was necessary for the reconnaissance.

"I'm afraid it's going to be a bit difficult, if there is a cave, or something, to get an idea of it without a light," Ginger pointed out. "I've no matches. All our things were taken away from us."

"I've got some," Biggles told him, remembering those

115

which, with his cigarettes, he had put in his pocket. "Take them, but go easy with them, and don't strike any in the open."

Ginger took the box, and slipping through an opening that had once been a window, crept stealthily along a wall towards his objective, while the others covered his advance with their rifles. Hearing nothing, seeing no sign of life, pausing sometimes to listen, Ginger kept close against the wall until he reached the trench, which gave him all the cover he needed for the rest of his journey to the stone. Actually, there were several paving-stones, and in spite of his confidence, in the deceptive half-light he was some minutes finding the right one. It was an exciting moment when he felt it give under his weight, for, of course, he had not the remotest idea of what was underneath.

The stone moved slowly but easily; when the pressure was removed it swung back into place, and for this reason he was in some doubt as to how to proceed. He didn't like the idea of descending into the unknown without being quite certain that he would be able to get back. A closer examination revealed that the stone turned on a central pivot; for a primitive contrivance it was a beautiful piece of precision work, but before entering the void Ginger made sure of his exit by the simple expedient of fixing a loose piece of stone so that the slab could not entirely close. Then, rather breathless, he groped inside with his hands. He was not surprised when they encountered a step, also of stone.

If there was one, he reasoned, there should be more. And in this he was correct; but it was not until he was well inside that he risked lighting a match. He held his breath while it flared up, for he had no idea of what lay before him. He was prepared for anything.

Actually, the result of his first survey, while the match lasted, was rather disappointing. As far as he could see, a flight of well-cut steps led down, perfectly straight, to a room, a chamber so large that he could not see the extremities of it. There was no furniture. The walls appeared to be bare. He went on to the bottom of the steps and lit another match.

In its light everything was exposed to view, and it

merely confirmed his first impression. He was in a large oblong room, the walls, floor and ceiling of which were of grey stone. At one end, the end farthest from the entrance, three broad, shallow steps led up to a dais, in the manner of an altar, on which squatted a hideous idol. It appeared to have been carved out of the living rock. Ginger went over to it, and by the light of the third match looked at it again. The image leered down at him, and he felt suddenly cold. For how many hundreds of years, perhaps thousands, it had been there, leering in the darkness, he did not know, but the effect of extreme antiquity affected him strangely. He struck yet another match, but there was nothing more to be seen. There was no door or passage leading to another room. If the treasure was in here, he thought, then they had been forestalled. It was certainly not there now, although it seemed likely that it had been there as late as 1937, or the explorer Roberts would not have carved his initials on the column.

It was a disappointing anti-climax, and feeling rather gloomy about the whole business, Ginger groped his way back up to the exit, from where, with due precautions, he returned to the house and told the others the result of his investigation.

"There's something funny about this," declared Biggles quietly. "Unless he was a first-class liar, Carmichael saw the treasure. So apparently did Roberts. Where has it gone? It seems very unlikely that anyone could have been on the plateau recently without the Tiger knowing about it, unless the explorers came as we did, by air, for they would have to come up Jacob's Ladder. Obviously, the Tiger didn't find the treasure, or he wouldn't be looking for it now—at least, I assume he's looking for it. I can't think what else he'd be looking for."

"Just a minute," put in Eddie. "There was some writing in the corner of the map. I imagine Roberts wrote it."

"What happened to this man Roberts?" asked Biggles curiously. "Why did he dispose of the map? Why didn't he take the treasure?"

"His Indian porters deserted him. In fact, they tried to poison him."

"So he couldn't carry the stuff?"

"That's right. It took him all his time to get back."

"But why didn't he return afterwards?"

"He died."

"How did these crooked partners of yours get hold of the map?"

"They bought it off Robert's widow—so they said."

"And this writing you just mentioned?"

"It was a list of instructions. I can't remember the words exactly, but there was something about a hinged stone—presumably the one Ginger discovered."

"Roberts definitely saw the treasure—with his own eyes?"

"Oh yes. He brought a gold cup home with him."

"Did you see it?"

"No. His widow sold it after he died."

"Hm." Biggles was silent for a moment. "I should like to have a look at this place," he announced.

"So should I," said Eddie.

"Then let's all go," suggested Biggles. "We shall be no worse off there than we are here—in fact, it might turn out to be a better hiding-place. If we could get hold of some food and water we could lie low there for a week if necessary, in which case the Tiger might think we had in some way got off the plateau. Let's go. We can always come back if we don't like it. No noise. We'll go across one at a time. If we bump into trouble, rally here. Ginger, you know the way, so you'd better go first."

Ginger, employing the same tactics as before, returned to the underground chamber. The others followed in turn, Biggles bringing up the rear. Everything remained quiet—from Biggles's point of view, suspiciously quiet. In spite of what he had said about the Tiger holding them in a trap by simply putting a guard on the stairway, he thought it was odd that no attempt had been made to dislodge them from the block of buildings in which they had sought refuge. Still, he did not overlook the fact that four desperate white men, armed with rifles, made a formidable force to capture or shoot down by sheer frontal attack.

Before going down through the trap-door Biggles made a short excursion to collect some tufts of dried grass: then, after a final survey of the scene, he followed the others into

118

the chamber and allowed the slab to sink slowly into place. As soon as he was inside he twisted the dried grass into a wisp—it could hardly be called a torch—and taking the matches from Ginger, set light to it. The grass blazed up brightly so that everything could be seen. Not that there was much to see.

Nobody spoke while the fire was alight. Biggles still had a little more grass, but as there seemed to be no point in burning it, he held it in reserve.

"Well, that's that," he murmured, sitting on the bottom step. "Did anyone notice anything interesting, or worth exploring?"

The others admitted that they had seen nothing worth mentioning.

"This is a funny business," resumed Biggles. "I still don't understand what became of the treasure."

"I wish I had the map," remarked Eddie. "There may have been something on it that I have forgotten. If there was, and the Tiger ever finds this place, he'll know just what to do."

"Well, there doesn't seem to be much *we* can do," returned Biggles.

Ginger started groping his way round the walls, knocking on the stones with his knuckles. "They sound solid enough," he observed.

"Lumps of stone, weighing half a ton apiece, would sound solid, even if there was a cavity behind," Biggles pointed out.

"What are we going to do?" asked Algy. "I can't see any point in staying here."

"There's not much point in going back to the house, if it comes to that," answered Biggles. "I don't want to be depressing, but I don't think we're in any shape to stay either here or in the house for more than another day. We might manage without food for a bit, but we can't do without water. I'm afraid that sooner or later we've got to risk breaking through the cordon, either by rushing the steps, or trying to get out over the rocks, the way I came in. I'll tell you what. I'll go and have a scout round."

"That sounds pretty dangerous to me," muttered Eddie dubiously.

Biggles laughed mirthlessly. "Whatever we do is likely to be dangerous. I'll go and make sure that the escarpment is guarded. Either way, I'll come back. If it isn't guarded we'll try to slip out."

"Why not all go?" suggested Ginger.

"Because four people are more likely to be seen than one, and the chances of making a noise become multiplied by four. No, this is a one-man job. I don't suppose I shall be very long. Here, Algy, you take the matches; you may need them."

Biggles groped his way up the steps. There was a faint gleam of star-spangled sky as he went through the exit; then it was blotted out as the stone sank into place. Silence fell.

For a long time nobody spoke in the chamber. There seemed to be nothing to say—or it may have been that they were all listening intently for the first sign of Biggles's return. In such conditions it is practically impossible to judge time correctly, but when Biggles had been gone for what Ginger thought must be nearly an hour, he commented on it.

"He's a long time," he said anxiously, almost irritably.

"I was thinking the same thing," admitted Algy. "If——"

Whatever he was going to say remained unsaid, for at that moment the silence was shattered by a deafening explosion. The chamber shuddered to the force of it. A moment later came the crash and spatter of debris raining down on the roof. It sounded like a roll of distant thunder.

Ginger flung himself flat, feeling sure that the whole place was about to collapse. This was purely instinctive, for he was beyond lucid thought. So were the others. The explosion would have been bad enough had it been expected, but coming as it did without warning, it was shattering. It took Ginger several seconds to convince himself that he had not been hurt. He was the first to speak.

"Are you fellows all right?" he asked in a strained voice.

The others answered that they were.

"What on earth was that?" continued Ginger.

"I don't know, but I'm going to find out," replied Algy, groping his way up the steps.

Some time passed, but he did not speak again, although the others could hear him making strange noises. He seemed to be grunting with exertion.

"What's wrong?" asked Eddie.

"Plenty," came Algy's voice in the darkness. "Either some rocks have fallen on the slab or else the explosion has jammed it. It won't move."

"You mean—we're shut in?" demanded Ginger.

"That's just what I do mean," answered Algy, rather unsteadily.

Ginger squatted down on the stone floor. "Not so good," he remarked.

"What are you grumbling about? You wanted adventure," Algy pointed out coldly. "Now you're getting it. I hope you're enjoying it—but I'm dashed if I am."

Biggles Makes a Capture

THE FIRST THING Biggles noticed when he left the underground chamber was that the moon was rising over the edge of the plateau. He had no time to weigh up the advantages and disadvantages of this, for as, lying flat, he began to worm his way towards the trench, he distinctly saw a dark shadow flit silently away from the side of the house which they had recently evacuated. An instant later a low mutter of voices reached his ears, but precisely where the sound came from he could not determine. The conversation was soon followed by the sound of retreating footsteps. That something was going on seemed certain, but there was no indication of what it was. Fearing that he may have been seen, he lay still for a little while, trusting to his ears to advise him of danger; but when nothing happened he felt that it was time he continued his reconnaissance.

With eyes and ears alert for danger, he reached the nearest house, and taking advantage of the deepest shadows, went on towards the ridge of rock which he could see silhouetted against the sky beyond the village. He reached the outlying boulders without incident, and there paused to survey the skyline for any movement that would reveal the position of sentries. His vigilance was rewarded when he saw the glow of a lighted cigarette. It was stationary. This at once fixed the position of at least one sentry, and Biggles was about to move forward on a course that would avoid him when a faint smell, borne on a slant of air, reached his nostrils and brought him to an abrupt halt. It was vaguely familiar, but it took him a second or two to identify it as the reek of smouldering saltpetre. Instantly realising the significance of it, he half rose up and looked behind him, hoped to discover the source of it. The next moment a column of flame shot into the air; simultaneously came the roar of an explosion, the blast of which flung him headlong. Knowing what to expect, he lay still with his hands over his head while clods of earth and pieces of rock rattled down around him and the acrid tang of dynamite filled the air.

As soon as the noise had subsided he looked back at the spot where the explosion had occurred, and saw, as he already suspected, that it was the block of houses in one of which they had first taken cover. The buildings were now a heap of ruins. It was easy enough to see what had happened. The enemy, fearing to make a frontal attack, had entered one of the rear houses and destroyed the whole block with a charge of dynamite.

Naturally, Biggles's first reaction to this unexpected event was one of thankfulness that they had left the house, otherwise they must have all been killed. That the enemy assumed this to be the case was made apparent by the way they now advanced, with much laughing and talking, from several directions. The sentries on the escarpment left their posts and joined their companions at the scene of the supposed triumph. In a few minutes the shattered houses were surrounded by groups of figures, some of which, Biggles saw with misgiving, were very near the underground chamber.

He waited to see what they would do, for upon this now depended his own actions. He was not particularly concerned about the others, although he guessed that the explosion must have given them a nasty shock. Being underground, they would be safe. He was not to know that falling masonry had piled itself on the entrance slab, making the opening of it from the inside impossible. His one fear was that Algy and Ginger would emerge in order to see what had happened, and so betray the secret hiding-place—as, indeed, might easily have happened had it been possible for them to get out. Biggles was relieved when nothing of the sort happened.

The question now arose in his mind, would a search be made at once for the bodies which were supposed to be under the ruins, or would the Tiger wait for daylight? The answer was provided when the Tiger began shouting orders, and the crowd started to disperse. As far as Biggles could gather, the Tiger had merely dismissed his men without giving any hint of his future plans. A number of figures, presumably the Tiger's personal party, remained near the ruins, and had it not been for this Biggles would probably have returned to the chamber forthwith. He did, in fact, wait for some time with this object in view, but when the Tiger showed no signs of leaving, he decided that it would be a good moment, an opportunity that might not occur again, to make contact with Dusky, who, if he did not soon show up, would presently be leaving the ravine. So Biggles decided that he would go down to him, tell him what had happened, recover his Express rifle and some biscuits, and then, if the Tiger had gone, return to the chamber. He thought it ought to be possible to do this before daylight.

His mind made up, he struck off towards the clump of prickly pear in order to leave the plateau as near as possible to the spot by which he had entered it. He was not so optimistic as to hope that he would be able to find his track through the chaos of rock, but he had a pretty good idea of the general direction of the ravine, and once he reached it there should be no great difficulty in finding Dusky.

Actually, he was some time finding the ravine, for it was not an easy matter to keep a straight course through the bewildering jumble of boulders; and when he did strike it he saw that he was above the point where he had left it. This did not worry him, however, and he started making his way towards the place where he imagined Dusky would be. When he reached it the old man was not there. He whistled softly, but there was no reply. Rather worried, he continued on towards the stairway, no great distance.

Had not he seen the moonlight glint on the barrel of the rifle there might have been an accident, for he realised suddenly that the rifle was covering him.

He dropped behind a rock. "Is that you, Dusky?" he asked sharply.

"Sure, massa, dat's me," answered Dusky with a gasp of relief. "I sure nearly shot you," announced the old man with engaging frankness.

"What are you doing here?" asked Biggles.

"When I hear all dat shootin' and bangin' I reckon you ain't comin' back no more, so I was jest off to fetch massa Carruthers. I'd have gone down the steps by now if dat trashy king hadn't come along."

"King?"

Dusky explained that a few minutes earlier he was about to descend the stairway when he heard someone approaching, coming down the steps. Withdrawing into the ravine, he saw, or thought he saw, the Tiger, with only two men, go past.

Biggles perceived that if the king had left the scene of the explosion shortly after he himself had left, he would have had ample time to reach the spot. He thought swiftly, wondering how this new aspect could be turned to his advantage. If Dusky was right, then the Tiger had probably gone down to his palace—with only two men. If he could be captured, he would be a valuable hostage. With the king in his hands, he could dictate to Bogat and his crew. He remembered also that the Tiger had the treasure map, which was a valuable document for more reasons than one. If he captured the king he would also gain possession of the map. It was a tempting proposition, and the only doubt in Biggles's mind was what the others would think when he did not return. Still, he thought they ought to be able to take care of themselves. Making up his mind quickly he moved towards the steps.

"Where you go now, massa?" asked Dusky.

"I'm going down to the valley to capture the king," answered Biggles shortly.

"You what—?" Dusky faltered. He shook his head sorrowfully, but followed as obediently as a dog.

The stairway was, as far as could be ascertained,

deserted, and Biggles hurried down, for time was an important factor. Reaching the valley, he surveyed the scene. Everything was, as he hoped, quiet. The only sign of activity was a light that came from the palace. With his rifle over his arm, Biggles strode towards it, trusting that if he were seen his disguise would see him through.

As he drew nearer he observed that the light came from the French window which gave access to the room in which he and Ginger had been trapped by the Tiger's pet snake. Suddenly a shadow moved across it, and he realised that a sentry was on duty. However, he went on into the garden and took cover behind a bush. It was now possible to see the sentry clearly. He carried a rifle at the slope.

Biggles leaned his Express against a bush and spoke quietly to Dusky. "We've got to get that fellow out of the way," he whispered. "Can you think of any way of bringing him here?"

Dusky scratched his head. "I dunno, massa, but I'll try." He whistled softly.

The sentry, who was pacing up and down, stopped abruptly.

"Who's there?" he called.

Biggles nudged Dusky, who whistled again.

The sentry, his curiosity aroused, began to walk slowly towards the spot. Dusky moved into the open where he could be seen. The sentry paused, then continued to move forward, his rifle at the ready.

"Who's that? What you doing here?" he asked sharply.

"I got a message," answered Dusky.

"Who for?"

"For you."

Upon this the sentry, seeing—as he thought—that he had only one man, a native, to deal with, proceeded with more confidence. He passed Biggles, and peered forward to see the face of the man in front of him. This was the moment for which Biggles had waited. The butt of his pistol came down on the sentry's head, and with a grunt the man collapsed at Dusky's feet. Biggles picked up the fallen rifle and thrust it into Dusky's hands.

"Stay here and watch him," he ordered, and moving

cautiously towards the building, saw what he had not previously noticed. The French window was open, probably on account of the heat.

Quietly, but without loss of time, taking his rifle with him, Biggles moved forward until he could see into the room. Two men were there, seated at a table with a bottle between them. One was Bogat and the other Chorro.

Biggles's first feeling was one of surprise; the second, disappointment; the third, mystification. Where was the Tiger? Bogat was still wearing his hat, as if he had only just arrived. Could Dusky have made a mistake?

While Biggles was still pondering the question Bogat spoke, and his first words explained the situation.

"No, the king is busy up top," he said. "When he heard that you'd arrived he sent me down instead to hear what you have to say. If you'd rather see him, or if it's something important, I'll take you up top."

Biggles understood. In the darkness Dusky had been mistaken. The man he had seen come down the steps was not the Tiger, but Bogat. Chorro had arrived from the coast, and the Tiger had sent Bogat down to get in touch with him.

Biggles was annoyed, for had he known the truth he would not have come down; but now that he was here, with the two men practically at his mercy, he felt that it would be a pity not to take advantage of the situation. He could not very well blame Dusky for the mistake; the old man had acted for the best. Still, the new state of affairs called for an adjustment of plan.

Biggles withdrew a little into the darkness to think the matter over. It would, he thought, be an easy matter to capture the Tiger's two right-hand men, but what was he to do with them? It did not take him long to see that there was only one thing he could do with them, and that was take them to the coast. This would mean leaving the others for longer than he originally intended. Still, if he went back up the steps and rejoined them now it was not easy to see what he could do single-handed. On the other hand, if he went to the coast and explained matters to Carruthers, the acting-Governor might lend him some extra men. He should be able to get back some time the next day. If Algy and the others remained where they were they should be safe.

So Biggles reasoned as he stood in the shadow of the palace, confronted, for the third time within a few hours, with a decision not easy to make. Successive unexpected events had made his original plan a thing of the past. However, he felt that by securing Bogat and Chorro and taking them to the coast he would have achieved the first step forward in his declared intention of breaking up the Tiger's gang.

With the rifle in the crook of his arm ready for instant use, Biggles strolled into the room.

"Good evening, gentlemen," he said evenly. "Keep quite still. It should hardly be necessary for me to warn you that if either of you make a sound I shall have to employ your own methods to discourage you. Keep your hands on the table."

The two men stared. Neither moved. Neither spoke. In the first place, at least, their obedience was probably due to shock. While they were still staring Biggles walked behind each in turn and removed his weapons.

"Now," he continued, "we're going for a walk. On your feet. Keep going. I shall be close behind you."

When they reached the spot where Dusky was waiting, Biggles gave him Bogat's rifle and ordered him to lead the way down to the forest, the first part of the journey to the *Wanderer*.

It was now bright moonlight, but so much had happened that Biggles had only a hazy idea of the time. He was anxious to reach the foot of the steps before dawn, because there was less chance of meeting anybody on the way.

As a matter of fact it was earlier than he thought, and he found it necessary to wait for some time at the bottom of the steps, for he dare not risk losing his two dangerous prisoners in the darkness of the forest, where, of course, the moonlight did not penetrate. As soon as there was sufficient light to see he gave the order to continue the march, Dusky still leading the way and he himself bringing up the rear. So far the two prisoners had been passive, but Biggles felt certain that Bogat, at least, would make an attempt to escape. Once he got off the trail into the forest he would be safe from pursuit, and Biggles repeated his warning as to what would happen if either prisoner attempted it. They trudged on in silence. It was broad daylight by the time they reached the river.

Now all this time Biggles had the advantage of knowing where they were going, whereas the prisoners did not. They hoped, no doubt, that camp would presently be made, in which case an opportunity for making a dash into the jungle might present itself. But as soon as the aircraft came into view—for in spite of Biggles's rough camouflage, it could be seen from a little distance—the manner of both prisoners changed. They must have realised that unless they did something quickly their minutes of opportunity were numbered. Once in the machine, and in the air, there could be no escape.

Not for an instant did Biggles relax his vigilance, for he knew that this was the crucial moment. He was in fact ready for almost anything; yet in spite of that he was not ready for what did happen.

When they were only a score of paces from the machine Dusky suddenly pulled up dead. For a moment or two he stood rigid, leaning slightly forward, his big nostrils twitching like a dog that catches the scent of its quarry. Then he turned his head slowly and looked at Biggles. His eyes were round with fear.

Even when he moved his lips, and opened them to speak, Biggles still had no idea of what the old man was going to say; but he sensed danger, and his muscles tightened as instinctively he braced himself. And as they all stood there, motionless, like a screen picture suddenly arrested in motion, the silence was broken by a curious sound, a sort of sharp *phut*.

Bogat started convulsively. Very slowly, as if it dreaded what it might find, his hand crept up to a face that had turned ashen, to where a tiny dart, not much larger than a darning needle, protruded. As his fingers touch it a wild scream burst from his lips, and he staggered back against a tree.

Chorro took one terrified look at him, and with the whimpering cry of a wounded dog, regardless of Biggles's order to stop, rushed into the forest.

129

Biggles raised his rifle, but he did not shoot. There was no need. For hardly had Chorro left the trail when there was a fierce crashing in the undergrowth, a crashing above which rose shrieks of terror. They ended abruptly.

Now all this had happened in less time than it takes to tell. Biggles knew, without Dusky's hoarse advice, that they had been ambushed by Indians, probably the same tribe that Bogat had so mercilessly attacked. He could do nothing for his prisoners. Chorro had disappeared, and it was not hard to guess his fate. Bogat was now on the ground, writhing and twisting in convulsions as the venom on the dart took effect.

Dusky panicked—which was hardly surprising. He fled back along the trail. Biggles followed, now concerned only with escape. He wondered vaguely whether it would be better to go back to the steps, or to try to reach the aircraft, although how this was to be done was not apparent. As he ran, wild shouts behind sent the parrots squawking into the air.

Dusky turned away from the trail like a hunted rabbit. Biggles followed blindly, not so much because he had any faith in his leadership—at least, in the present circumstances—as because he did not want to lose him. Presently he found himself splashing through mud, and saw the tall reeds that fringed the river just ahead. Dusky made for a tree on which the limbs grew low. Flinging aside his rifle, he went up it like a monkey. Biggles went after him, but kept his rifle, looping it over his shoulder by the sling to leave his hands free for climbing.

He thought Dusky would never stop going up, and for some absurd reason the memory of Jack and the Beanstalk flashed into his mind. The ground was about a hundred feet below when Dusky suddenly disappeared and Biggles, still following, found himself in a strange new world. They had arrived, so to speak, in a new jungle, a jungle with a fairly level floor from which sprang orchids and ferns, with great growths of moss and lichen.

Now, Biggles had heard of these different "layers" of forest, raised one above the other, but this was the first time he had ever seen one, and he looked about with interest. It was easy to see how they were formed. Branches fell, but instead of falling to the ground, they were caught by the branches below them. Across these in turn fell other branches, twigs and leaves, to form eventually a substantial carpet. On this carpet seeds fell from the flowering tree-tops. Others were dropped by birds. These took root and flourished for a time; then, dying, the seedlings collapsed, to give extra thickness to the mat of rotting debris. Over a period of centuries this mat became as firm as the solid earth far beneath, and supported a flora and fauna of its own. Here among the green tree-tops dwelt birds, and rats, and other small creatures.

Biggles was recalled from his contemplation of this pleasant scene by Dusky, who whispered, "We hide here."

Biggles nodded. He was in no mood to argue. All the same, he began to regret that he had left the others. He wondered what they were doing. Could he have seen them he would have been a good deal more disturbed in his mind than he was.

Desperate Diversions

I F BIGGLES SUPPOSED that Algy, Ginger and Eddie were sitting quietly in the underground chamber waiting for him to come back—and there was no reason why he should think otherwise—he would have been wrong. Very wrong. Things had happened Several things.

They began soon after Algy's discovery that, as a result of the explosion, the stone over the exit had jammed. At least, that is what they thought. As a matter of fact, a block of masonry had fallen on it. Masonry had fallen all over the place. Comparatively speaking, this particular piece was not heavy, but it was of sufficient weight to upset the finely adjusted mechanism of the pivot and so prevent the slab from being tilted open from the inside. Those below it did not know this. As Algy remarked, "The thing has stuck." They were not at first unduly perturbed, for they assumed that Biggles would return and do something about it. But when presently the sound of many footsteps could be heard overhead, Algy began to get worried. This was, of course, when the Tiger and his men gathered round the scene of the explosion.

Conversing in low tones, the comrades tried to visualise the scene outside, and as a result of their combined imaginations they arrived fairly near to the truth.

"They've either brought up a cannon and shelled the

place, or else blown it up with a stick of dynamite," declared Algy.

"I only hope they didn't get Biggles at the same time," muttered Ginger.

"He'd been gone a fair while," Algy pointed out. "He should have got clear."

"We shall have to wait until he comes back."

"We should have done that in any case," reminded Algy.

Time passed, a long time, and still Biggles did not return. There were no longer any sounds outside.

"Surely it's time he was back?" murmured Ginger. "This is awful, sitting here doing nothing."

"I'm afraid you're right," agreed Algy. "If everything had gone according to plan he should have been back by now. It begins to look as if something went wrong."

"What can we do about it?"

"Nothing. At least, I can't think of anything. Have you any ideas, Eddie?"

Eddie answered that he had not. "I must have been nuts to set out on this jaunt with a pair of cheap crooks," he added disgustedly—which made it clear how he felt about the whole business.

"How about striking a match and having a look at the slab?" he suggested presently. "Perhaps we shall be able to see what's happened." They had of course been sitting in the dark.

"Yes, we might do that," agreed Algy. "But we shall have to go steady with the matches—there aren't many left."

"Why is it nobody seems to have any matches when they are really needed?" remarked Eddie bitterly.

"I'll see it never happens to me again," declared Ginger. "Before I set out on another trip I'm going to have a special belt made, one to go under my shirt. It will have little pockets all round it. In them I shall carry everything I've always wanted when I haven't had them—a box of matches, and an electric torch, a penknife with all sorts of gadgets in it, chocolates, string——"

"A few bombs and a Tommy gun," sneered Algy. "Pity you didn't think of it earlier. Stop romancing. Let's get down to brass tacks. I'm going to strike a match, so get ready to have a look round."

As he spoke he struck the match. It flared up, dazzling them. As their eyes grew accustomed to the light they examined the slab eagerly, but there was nothing to indicate the cause of the trouble. Just as the flame was expiring a wild yell from Eddie nearly made Ginger fall off the step. The match went out.

"What's wrong? What are you yelling about?" snapped Algy.

"It's gone?"

"Gone? Who's gone? I mean, what's gone?"

"The idol."

"You're crazy! Where could it go?"

"I tell you it's gone," insisted Eddie. "I happened to glance that way. It's no longer there."

"Strike another match, Algy," put in Ginger nervously. "I don't like the idea of an image prowling about."

In his haste Algy dropped all the matches, and several seconds passed—much to Ginger's irritation—before they could be collected.

"For the love of Mike get a move on," he growled.

Another match flared, and they all stared in the direction of the image. One glance was enough. Eddie was right. It was no longer there.

With one accord, prompted by mutual curiosity, they started walking towards the place where it had been, but before they were half-way the match went out. Still, they had seen enough to give them an idea of what had happened.

"Strike another match," urged Ginger.

"We can't go on striking matches at this rate," protested Algy.

"Wait a minute. I'll tear a strip off my shirt," offered Ginger. There came a noise of tearing material. "All right, go ahead," he resumed. "I hope the stuff will burn."

Another match blazed, and Ginger lighted the piece of material that he now held in his hands. "That's better," he said, as it flared up.

It was now possible to see precisely what had happened. The explosion had evidently been more severe than they

134

had supposed, for there were several cracks in the walls and ceiling. With these they were not concerned. Their attention was riveted on a more interesting development. At first they could not understand what had become of the idol, but as they drew near they saw that the shock of concussion had caused it to tilt forward, revealing a square aperture behind it, a hole into which the base of the idol had previously fitted.

In order to reach this opening Algy had to climb on the back of the idol, but as soon as he touched it it swung still lower in a manner that explained how it operated. The idol was, in fact, a door, hinged at the bottom by a balancing device similar to the one that worked the slab above. So perfectly poised was the idol that the slightest pressure was sufficient to move it, but what hidden spring actuated it could not be discovered. With such precision did the ponderous stone with the carved face fit into the recess behind it, that, had not the explosion exposed the secret, it would not have been suspected.

"This is getting interesting," murmured Algy.

"You bet it is," declared Ginger enthusiastically. "Go ahead. Let's see what's inside."

"You've got the light, go ahead yourself," invited Algy.

"Say, why argue? Let's all go," put in Eddie. And in a moment they were all standing in the dark doorway, Ginger holding up the piece of burning stuff in order to throw the light as far as possible.

As a means of illumination the strip of shirt left much to be desired, but in its smoky yellow glow they saw three broad steps that led down into another chamber, a long, low room with what appeared to be heaps of debris piled at intervals on the floor. There was only one piece of furniture—a curiously carved chair.

"There doesn't seem to be anything to get worked up about," observed Ginger in a disappointed voice, as they advanced slowly down the steps.

As Ginger trod on the bottom step it seemed to give under his weight, and he fell back with a cry of alarm. The light went out. Simultaneously, the chamber echoed to a dull, hollow boom.

Algy needed no invitation to relight the piece of rag. At

first glance there appeared to be no change in the scene, and it was Eddie, who happened to glance behind him, who called attention to what had occurred. The entrance had disappeared. The idol had swung back into place.

"When I was a kid," announced Eddie sadly, "my Ma always swore that my inquisitiveness would be the death of me. I guess she was right. Unless we can find the gadget that tips old frosty-face, I reckon we're here for keeps."

"Let's have a look before we try to find it," suggested Algy. "You may not have noticed it, but that idol fits into its socket like a piston into a cylinder. So does the outside slab. In that case, how does it happen that the air in here is so fresh? Look at the light. You don't suppose it would burn like that if the chamber wasn't ventilated somehow?"

"You're right," agreed Ginger, sinking into the chair. In an instant he was on his back, for the chair had collapsed in a cloud of dust. It did not break; it just crumbled, like tinder.

"That chair must have been standing there an awful long time," said Eddie slowly.

Ginger, sneezing, sat on a pile of debris. It sank a little under his weight, and gave a soft metallic clink. A curious expression came over his face as he picked up a handful of the stuff. He said no word, but turning an amazed face to the others, allowed the pieces to drop one by one from his hand. They fell with a dull clink.

"For the love of Mike," breathed Eddie. "It's metal."

Ginger laughed hysterically. "Feel the weight of it," he cried. "It's gold!"

In a moment they were all on their knees examining their find, and soon established that the objects were not coins, but an extraordinary collection of small carved objects, trinkets, flowers, ears of corn, and the like. Digging into the pile, Algy pulled out a drinking-mug made in the form of a potato.

"It's the treasure all right," he said in a strained voice, just as the light burnt out. "Unfortunately, it's no earthly use to us at the moment, but it's nice to know it's here. Rip another strip off your shirt," he ordered. "Let's see about getting out of this trap."

Ginger obliged, and by mutual consent they returned

to the steps, from where they made a close examination of the back of the idol. They tried coaxing it open, and failing in this, they tried force. But it was no use. They could see the cracks that marked the dimensions of the opening clearly enough, but nothing they could do would widen them.

"We're wasting our time," said Eddie in a melancholy voice.

"Don't you believe it," returned Ginger. "The old priests, or whoever made this dugout, wouldn't fix the thing without making some way of opening it from the inside. There's a trick in it. All we've got to do is to discover it."

"If they were cute enough to make a trap like this you can bet your sweet life the trick won't be easy to solve," said Eddie. "Only those in the secret could get in and out."

"What I should like to know," remarked Algy, "is where the fresh air is coming from. It can't percolate through solid stone."

"You're dead right," affirmed Eddie. "There must be a hole, or a feed-pipe somewhere. And I'll tell you something else. Even if there is a hole the air couldn't get in if we were below the level of the ground."

"What are you talking about?" demanded Ginger. "Of course we're below the level of the ground. We came downstairs."

"Unless the guys who built this hide-out installed a mechanical air-conditioning plant, which I'm not prepared to believe, then I say the air is coming in from some point below us," declared Eddie.

"I think you're right," agreed Algy thoughtfully. "If we can find the hole we shall know more about it."

Abandoning the sealed doorway, they set about exploring the chamber, starting with the walls; but everywhere the massive stones of which the chamber was composed fitted so perfectly that the task seemed hopeless. Eddie turned his attention to the floor, dropping on his knees to examine it more closely.

"You've got to remember that the ancients were clever engineers, but even so, their work was limited to simple mechanics," he remarked. "They had a primitive idea of hydraulics and levers, so——" The voice broke off abruptly. It was followed by a soft thud.

Algy looked round. So did Ginger. Then they stared at each other.

"Hi! Eddie!" shouted Ginger.

There was no answer.

Ginger turned wondering eyes to Algy. "He's—he's gone!" he gasped.

"D'you think I'm blind?" sneered Algy with bitter sarcasm, which revealed the state of his nerves. "Where was he when he disappeared?"

Ginger shook his head. "I don't know. I was looking at the wall."

"All right. Let's not get excited. There's dust on the floor. When we find the place where it has been disturbed we shall know where he was when he did the disappearing act."

"I hope he isn't hurt," muttered Ginger.

"He's probably groping about on the wrong side of one of these slabs, trying to get back," asserted Algy, taking the light from Ginger's hand and starting to explore the flagstones which formed the floor.

"This is the place," he announced presently. "Apart from the dust, the cracks round this slab are wider than the others."

"Perhaps it tilts, like the one up top," suggested Ginger.

"That must be the answer, otherwise Eddie couldn't very well have fallen through," replied Algy. "Yes, that's it," he went on quickly. "The dust on this slab has disappeared. It probably fell into the hole, or whatever there is underneath, when Eddie went through. We're getting warm. I expect it's a case of applying weight to one particular spot. The most likely place would be near the edge, just here—Hi!"

Ginger grabbed Algy by the legs as the stone tilted suddenly and he started to slide. He nearly went in head first, and probably would have done had not Ginger dragged him back. As they struggled clear the stone swung back into place.

"Why did you let the hole close up again?" asked Ginger in a disappointed voice.

"Don't worry about that. We know the trick now," answered Algy breathlessly. "I don't want to land on my skull. We'll take this slowly: and as the trap closes automatically we'd better jam it open with something, otherwise it may close behind us and prevent us from getting back."

Ginger went to one of the heaps of treasure and returned with what looked like a wand, or sceptre. "This ought to do," he said.

"Fine," agreed Algy. "Slip it in the crack when the stone moves. As soon as the crack is wide enough we'll drop a match in to see how deep the hole is underneath— if there is a hole."

By the light of a match they ascertained that there was a drop, but only of about six feet; and the first thing they saw was Eddie lying crumpled up at the bottom, evidently unconscious.

Algy dropped down to him. There was no other way. Originally there had been a wooden ladder, but it now lay mouldering in a heap of dust. While Algy was examining Eddie, Ginger observed that the newly discovered cavity bore no likeness to the room they were in. It was more like an artificial cave, with the sides left rough. He also remarked a definite draught of air, refreshingly cool.

"How is he?" he called from above.

"He's got a nasty bruise on the forehead. He must have landed on his head; the blow knocked him out, but I don't think it's serious."

"Is that a room or a tunnel you're in?"

Algy held up the match and looked round. "It's a tunnel," he said. "You'd better come down. Jam the flags open so that we can get back if necessary."

Ginger dropped into the cave. "I say! A disturbing thought has just occurred to me," he remarked.

"What is it?"

"If Biggles comes back and finds no one in the chamber he'll wonder what on earth has become of us."

Algy clicked his tongue. "I'm afraid he'll have to wonder," he muttered wearily.

Carruthers Takes a Hand

THEIR FEARS IN THIS RESPECT, however, had they but known it, were groundless. Biggles was miles away, sitting in a sylvan paradise between earth and heaven, wondering what to do next. Dusky, being a man of the country, was concerned only with the immediate danger—the Indians, who could be heard laughing and shouting some distance away.

"I'm glad they chose Bogat for a target, and not me," remarked Biggles.

"Dey know Bogat. Dey want him for a long time. Dey take you for an Indian."

Biggles thought that this was probably the correct explanation. Not being a hypocrite, he made no pretence of being sorry for the brutal Bogat, or the treacherous Chorro, who had got no more than their deserts. An idea struck him.

"Is this carpet firm enough to walk on?" he inquired.

"Sure, massa."

"There's no risk of falling through?"

"No risk," declared Dusky confidently. "This stuff thirty or forty feet thick, maybe more."

"In that case we ought to be able to work our way along so as to get above the aeroplane. The river will serve as a guide."

Dusky shook his head. "If we walk, dem old parrots

will set up a squawking and tell the Indians where we are. Better if we wait. Presently de Indians go."

"Won't they smash the machine?"

"Dey too afraid to go near it," said Dusky definitely. "Dey tink, maybe, it's a new god."

Biggles was not so sure of this, but he was content to rely on Dusky's judgement. After all, he reflected, the old man had spent most of his life among the Indians, and should know their habits.

"Did you know the Indians were there?" asked Biggles, while they were waiting. He remembered that Dusky had stopped before the Indians had revealed their presence.

"Sure, massa."

"How did you know?"

"I smelled dem," explained Dusky simply.

Biggles nodded. He was prepared to believe anything. That Dusky had judged the situation correctly was presently proved when the Indians passed along the trail, in single file and in silence. As soon as they had disappeared into the dim corridors of the forest Dusky announced that it was safe to move. He did not descend straight to the ground, but kept to the tree-tops, picking his way carefully, with Biggles following. They were soon escorted by parrots and monkeys, which, coming close, but taking care to keep out of reach, set up a hideous clamour. Evidently they resented the intrusion into their domain, and left the invaders in no doubt as to their disapproval.

In several places there were holes in the floor, usually near the trunks of trees, such as the one through which they had made an entrance, and Dusky took care to keep well away from them. Eventually, however, he selected one, and stamping with his feet to make sure that he was on a branch, worked his way towards the hole. He pointed, and Biggles, to his infinite relief, saw the *Wanderer* almost immediately below. There was no sign of any damage.

Getting down to the ground was tricky and hot work, and Biggles was not a little relieved to stand once more on terra firma. Watching the undergrowth closely, and with his rifle at the ready, he hurried to the machine, which, to his great satisfaction, appeared to be precisely as he had

141

left it. Leaving Dusky on guard, he tore off the flimsy camouflage and prepared to cast off.

"Okay, Dusky, come aboard," he said in a tired voice, for strain, exertion, lack of sleep, and the humid atmosphere were beginning to tell. He was weary, hungry and thirsty, not to say dirty.

"Which way we go, massa?" asked Dusky anxiously.

"I'm just wondering," returned Biggles frankly, for now that the moment for departure had come he found himself in doubt. Two courses were open. The others, he knew, would be anxious about him, and he had an uncomfortable feeling that he had left them in the lurch. He had not stuck to his plan—not that this was entirely his fault. Algy and Ginger would no doubt agree that he had done the right thing when they knew what had happened, but in the meantime they would be worried. Nevertheless, it was not easy to see how he could rejoin them—anyway, until night fell. But apart from his he felt that the wisest course would be to go down the river and tell Carruthers what had happened. He might be able to make a suggestion. If not, Biggles reasoned, he would have to come back and carry on the war single-handed.

"We're going down the river," he told Dusky abruptly, as he made up his mind.

He started the engines and took off with a vague feeling of surprise that at last something was going according to order. He half expected the engines to break down. Indeed, on the journey to the coast he listened to their note with as much anxiety as he could ever remember, for if they let him down now he hardly dared think what the fate of the others would be.

The engines did not let him down, and he offered up a silent prayer of thankfulness when the sea came into view. In twenty minutes, leaving Dusky in charge of the aircraft, he was in the presence of the acting-Governor.

Carruthers looked him up and down with real concern.

"I say, old man, you are in a mess," he said sympathetically. "You need a bath, a——"

Biggles broke in. "I know. There are a lot of things I need, but I haven't time to attend to them now. Things have been happening—they're still happening, and I've got to get a move on. My friends don't know I'm here—but I'd better give you a rough idea of what has happened. While I'm doing that you might get me a spot of something to eat."

Carruthers sent his servant for a drink and some sandwiches, and these Biggles consumed as he told his story as concisely as possible.

"By Jingo! You have been having a time," exclaimed the acting-Governor when Biggles had finished. "What do you want me to do?"

"To tell the truth, I don't know," confessed Biggles. "I thought you might be able to make a suggestion. After all, we're working under you, and apart from personal considerations, I don't want to do the wrong thing."

"We've got to rescue your friends and this American, and, if possible, arrest the Tiger."

"That's it," agreed Biggles. "We'll grab these two crooks Warren and Schmitt at the same time. They deserve hanging for abandoning young Rockwell in the jungle. The trouble is, I can't be in two places at once. I rarely ask for assistance, but this seems to be a case where a little help would be worth a deal of sympathy."

"That's what I was thinking," murmured Carruthers, his lips parting in a faint smile.

"Do you really mean that?" asked Biggles sharply.

"I might snatch a couple of days off to help you to clean up. If I could, what would you suggest?"

"Now you're talking," said Biggles eagerly. "You see, I can't be at both ends of that infernal stairway at the same time. The Tiger has got a guard posted at the top, to keep us trapped up there—at least, that's what he thinks. If we had some men at the bottom of the steps we could keep *him* trapped. Otherwise even if we landed an army on the plateau, he'd simply bolt down the steps and disappear into the forest. How many native men can you spare?"

"Ten or a dozen—native police, of course. They're good fellows."

"Got a machine-gun?"

"I could get one."

Biggles thought quickly. "Two good men under a reliable
143

N.C.O., with a machine-gun, could hold the bottom of the stairway against an army. Three or four others arriving suddenly on the plateau, with another machine-gun, should be enough to stampede the Tiger's half-baked gang. Remember, I've already got three men up there. Let me see, by unloading most of my stores, at a pinch I could transport ten people up the river, including myself. Ten should be enough. We could land at the place where I just took off and unload Dusky, an N.C.O. and two men, with a machine-gun. Dusky would act as guide. He could show them where to place the gun so that it would cover the steps. Are you seriously thinking of coming?"

"Certainly."

"Good. Very well. You and I, and four others, would take off again and land on the plateau, and make a rush for this underground chamber I told you about. The idea of that would be to let my friends out. We should then have a force of nine men, which should be plenty. When the Tiger sees you he'll guess the game's up and bolt for the steps. His gang will follow him. We shall then have the whole bunch between two fires, and unless he's a lunatic he'll surrender. Believe me, that stairway is no place to fight a defensive action."

Carruthers nodded. "That sounds a good plan. When shall we start?"

"The sooner the better. How soon could you be ready?"

"In an hour."

"Fine. I'll refuel, have a bath, and meet you at the river in an hour from now. That will be one o'clock. If all goes well we ought to be back up the river by five— just nice time. There will be an hour or two of daylight left."

"That suits me," agreed Carruthers.

An hour later the heavily loaded aircraft, after a long run, took off and headed back up the river. Carruthers, with a service rifle across his knees, occupied the spare seat next to Biggles. Behind, packed in the cabin, was the little force of fighting men, all of whom were making their first trip in the air.

Biggles did not trouble about height—not that he could

have gone very high with such a full load even if he had wanted to. Generally speaking, he followed the river, so that he would be able to land his human freight safely should the emergency arise.

After some time the first landing-place, the bend where Bogat and Chorro had met their deaths, came into view, and Biggles set the *Wanderer* down gently on the water. Here four men were disembarked—Dusky, a sergeant, and two policemen. In addition to their small arms, they carried a Vickers machine-gun. They knew just what to do, for their part in the operation had been explained to them before the start. Under Dusky's guidance they were to proceed to the foot of the stairway and take up a position covering it. Anyone attempting to come down was to be arrested.

Biggles watched them file up the forest trail, and then, with an easier load, took off and headed for the plateau.

He tried to visualise what would happen when he landed. As he worked it out, the Tiger and his white associates would suppose that he was alone, in which case their mistake might cost them dear. Actually, he was not particularly concerned whether the Tiger fought or fled. His immediate concern was to get to the underground chamber and relieve Algy, Ginger and Eddie from their tiresome ordeal.

By air it was only a short distance to the plateau. Biggles did not waste time circling, for he knew there were no obstructions to be cleared. Lowering his wheels, he made for the spot he had chosen on the previous occasion.

"Tell your fellows to be ready to bundle out smartly as soon as the machine stops," he told Carruthers. "We're likely to come under fire right away, so get the machine-gun in action as quickly as possible. I don't think the Tiger will face it."

"Leave it to me," rejoined Carruthers quietly.

As he glided down to land Biggles could see men running from the village and many faces staring upward. It appeared as if the arrival of the machine had caused something like consternation. At the distance, however, he could not distinguish the Tiger.

The wheels touched; the machine rocked a little, and then ran on to a safe if bumpy landing. Kicking on hard rudder, and at the same time giving the engines a burst of throttle, Biggles guided the machine towards an outcrop of rock which he thought would make good cover. As soon as the *Wanderer* stopped he switched off, and grabbing his rifle jumped down. The others poured out behind him. Shots were already flicking up the dust, so the men, under Carruthers' leadership, made a dive for the rocks and there assembled the machine-gun.

About a dozen of the Tiger's men, led by the Tiger himself, were by this time sprinting towards the aircraft; but as the machine-gun started its devastating chatter they acted as Biggles expected they would. They turned and fled, leaving two of their number on the ground. Biggles picked off another man and then jumped to his feet.

"Come on! Let's get after them," he said crisply.

But now things took a surprising turn, a turn for which Biggles thought he should have been prepared, but as a matter of fact the possibility had not occurred to him. The labourers, who were really nothing less than slaves, were working in the trench. Biggles had noticed them before he landed, but they did not come into his calculations. It seemed, now, as if they suddenly realised that deliverance was at hand. They were nearly all natives from the coast, and perhaps they recognised Carruthers' spotless white uniform. Be that as it may, with one accord, and with a wild yell, they leapt out of the trench and attacked their masters, using as weapons the tools they held in their hands. Biggles saw the gang-boss go down under a rain of blows from picks and shovels. The survivors of this onset, the Tiger among them, bolted for the steps, pursued by a yelling crowd. Some, in their desperate haste to escape, threw away their rifles.

"What on earth is happening?" cried Carruthers.

"It looks as if the Tiger's slaves have decided to take a hand," answered Biggles grimly.

They could do nothing to prevent the massacre that followed. for they were still a good two hundred yards away, and the slaves were between them and the fugitives.

146

Biggles ran on, followed by the others, hoping to save life if it were possible, and anxious to get to the chamber.

Just before he reached it he saw a fearful sight. Five or six brawny natives, fleeter of foot than the rest, overtook the two white men, Warren and Schmitt, at the head of the stairway. The hunted men screamed as hands fell on them and pulled them down. Carruthers, seeing what was likely to happen, shouted, but he might as well have saved his breath. For a moment there was a knot of struggling figures. Then they separated, and the two white men, clutching at the air, swung out over the awful void. Then they disappeared from sight, their screams growing fainter as they plunged to destruction.

Biggles left the rest to Carruthers. Feeling a trifle sick, he dashed to the chamber, and saw, for the first time, the effect of the explosion. He realised at once that the others must have been trapped.

He beckoned to some of the ex-labourers who were standing about talking in excited groups and made them clear the masonry. As soon as the slab was exposed he opened it.

"Hullo there! " he called cheerfully.

There was no answer.

Biggles felt his heart miss a beat. He went down the first few steps and struck a match, holding the light above his head. His fears were at once confirmed. The chamber was empty. And there he stood, flabbergasted, until the match burnt his fingers.

"Hullo! " he shouted again, in a voice that had suddenly become hoarse.

But there was no reply.

Slowly, hardly able to believe his eyes, he made his way back up the steps to the fresh air.

Carruthers appeared. "What's the matter?" he asked quickly, noting the expression on Biggles's face.

"They're gone," said Biggles in a dazed voice.

"Gone?" echoed Carruthers incredulously. "Where could they have gone?"

Biggles shrugged his shoulders helplessly. "Don't ask me," he said bitterly. "I'm no magician."

Unexpected Meetings

BIGGLES MIGHT WELL have wondered what had become of Algy, Ginger and Eddie; and, as the idol had swung back into place, he might have searched for a long time without finding them. The earth had—as near as may be—opened and swallowed them up.

Eddie was a long time recovering from his fall, for only on the screen do people who have been stunned by a blow on the head recover in a few seconds. Algy and Ginger could do little to help him. They had not even any water. All they could do was squat beside him, rubbing his hands and fanning his face, at the same time debating whether they should try to carry him down the cave which they could see stretched for some distance—how far they did not know. It appeared to plunge down towards the centre of the earth.

They lost all count of time; indeed, they did not even know whether it was day or night when Eddie, after a few weak groans, eventually opened his eyes. Once consciousness returned he made fairly good progress, and presently was well enough to ask what had happened. He himself had no recollection beyond groping about on the floor looking for a trap-door.

"You found it," Algy told him with humorous sarcasm. "Having found it, you dived through and landed on your head."

Eddie struggled into a sitting position. "Where are we?"

"Ask me something easier," returned Algy wearily. "Still, if you're well enough to get on your feet we'll try to find out. It's no use going back, so we may as well go forward."

Now, all this time Ginger had kept a small fire going by tearing pieces off his shirt, with the result that there was very little of the garment left.

Eddie got up, rather unsteadily, while Ginger recklessly tore the remaining piece of shirt into strips to provide illumination. With this improvised torch he led the way, the others following, Eddie leaning on Algy's arm.

For some time nothing happened. The cave, a rough, narrow tunnel just high enough to enable them to stand upright, took a winding course downward at a steep angle. It seemed to go on interminably, but then suddenly opened out into a tremendous cavity in the earth, not unlike a cathedral. Enormous stalactites, like rows of organ-pipes, dropped from the roof to met spiky stalagmites that sprang upwards from the floor. From all around came the faint drip, drip, drip, of water, an eerie sound in such a place.

"Now what have we struck?" asked Ginger in an awed voice, looking round. He took a pace forward, but backed hastily.

"What's wrong?" asked Algy.

"The floor's soft."

"What do you mean—soft?"

"What I say. It feels like mud. It won't bear my weight."

Algy stepped forward and tested it. "You're right," he said slowly. "We seem to have struck a confounded bog."

"It looks as if we shan't be able to get any farther."

"Just a minute," put in Eddie. "Of course, there's always a chance that the bog has only been formed in recent years, but if it was always here, then surely there must be a way across, otherwise there would be no point in making the cave."

"That's a reasonable argument," agreed Algy. "All the same, I can't see any bridge." He began exploring the mud with his feet. "Just a minute, what have we here?" he cried. "It feels like a lump of rock just under the surface."

Ginger tried it. "That's what it is," he said, standing on

149

it. Groping with his foot, he found another. "That's it," he went on. "There are stepping-stones, but either they've sunk or the mud has risen and covered them. Let's see if we can get across."

"Gosh! I don't think much of this," muttered Algy as he followed. "What about you, Eddie? Can you manage?"

"Yes, I reckon so," answered Eddie, holding on to the wall for support. He drew his hand away sharply. "It's all right," he went on quickly. "It's only water. It's collected in a sort of basin in the rock. There must be a flaw, a fissure, in the rock, that lets the rain water in from above."

"Water!" gasped Ginger. "Let's have a drink. My throat's like dust."

In a moment they were all drinking greedily out of their cupped hands.

"That's better," exclaimed Ginger, rinsing his grimy face.

"You're sure right," agreed Eddie. "I feel a heap better for that."

They now proceeded again, Ginger, carrying the flame, leading the way. Several times a false step got him into difficulties. Once he stepped off the path and sank up to the waist in slime. Algy had hard work to pull him out, while all around the disturbed area the mud quaked and threw up huge noisome bubbles.

"Phew! What a stink," muttered Ginger disgustedly. "We ought to have brought masks," he added, trying to make light of the incident.

A moment later Eddie exclaimed, "You're right at that."

"About what?"

"Gas masks. My head's beginning to swim. There's sulphur in this gas. Push on, but don't fall in again, or you'll send up more gas."

Ginger needed no second invitation, and it was with a shout of relief that he saw the stepping-stones ahead protruding above the mud. Once they could see them, progress became faster, and it was not long before they arrived at what appeared to be a continuation of the cave, although it was now much larger.

Ginger turned, and holding up the flame in such a way

that it burned more brightly, took a last look at the sub-
terranean mere.

"I say, you fellows, what's that?" he asked in a startled
voice. "I mean—that shadow—over there. It seems to be
coming towards us."

The others turned and looked, and saw, as Ginger had
remarked, that a broad dark shadow was moving across
the morass towards them. The strange thing about it was
that it did not maintain an even rate of progress. It seemed
to dart forward a little way, then pause, then come on
again.

"Say! I don't like the look of that," said Eddie. "What
could cause a shadow in here?"

"That isn't a shadow," answered Algy in a hushed
whisper. "It's something—alive. I believe it's thousands of
insects of some sort. Yes, by gosh, that's it. Just look at
'em. They look like whacking great water-spiders. What
do they call those big spiders? Tarantulas. Their bite is
poisonous." He ended on a shrill note.

The others did not wait to confirm this. With one accord
they turned about and fled up the cave.

After going a little way Ginger looked over his shoulder.
"Look out!" he yelled. "They're coming!"

They blundered on. There was no longer any question
of going back.

"The next time you want to go adventuring, my lad,
you'll go alone," panted Algy once, viciously.

It was more by luck than judgement that Ginger spotted
the opening—or at least one opening, for there may have
been others. They were not even thinking of one, for the
cave still went downwards. Ginger happened to look up a
side turning, and noticed a ghostly grey glow. He pulled
up short.

"What's that?" he shouted.

The others stopped and looked. For a moment silence
reigned.

"It's daylight!" yelled Algy.

There was a rush for the spot. Algy reached it first, and
gave a cry of disappointment when he saw that the light
came through a narrow crack only a few inches wide,
although it was a yard or more long. A mouse might have

A gasp of horror broke from his lips when he saw the tarantulas

got through it, but nothing larger. Beyond, showing as a strip of blue silk, was the sky. It was obvious that the crack was merely a flaw in the rock, due, no doubt, to the effect of wind and rain on the outside.

Ginger, holding up the light, looked behind, and a gasp of horror broke from his lips when he saw the vanguard of the tarantulas only a few yards away.

Algy saw them too, and it was in sheer desperation that he flung himself against the rock, near the crack. He had no genuine hope that it would widen sufficiently to allow him to go through, consequently he was utterly unprepared for what happened. The whole rock gave way under his weight, and after a vain attempt to save himself, he fell through behind it. The next moment he was clutching wildly at anything as he slid down a short but steep slope to what seemed certain destruction, for all he could see below him was a fearful void. A little avalanche of rocks preceded him to the brink. Loose boulders followed him down. He gave himself up for lost.

When his heels struck solid ground he could hardly believe his good fortune. Then, not before, did he see where he was. He was on the stairway. On either hand ran the narrow cornice. Even then he nearly went over the edge, for a piece of rock, catching him in the small of the back, sent him sprawling. He fell across the path with his legs in space. With frantic haste he drew them in, caring little that his rifle went spinning into the void.

Now Ginger's startled face had appeared at the aperture behind Algy, so he had seen everything that had happened. He also saw something which Algy did not see. Happening to glance up the steps, he saw to his amazement and alarm that somebody was coming down—running down. There was no need to look twice to ascertain who it was. It was the Tiger. Ginger let out a yell of warning.

"Here! Grab this!" he shouted, and allowed his rifle to slide down the slope.

At this moment he in turn was warned by Eddie that the tarantulas were on their heels, so half slipping and half sliding, he followed the rifle to the steps. Eddie came down behind him, and nearly knocked him over the edge. By the time they got down to him, Algy was covering the

Tiger, who appeared to be unarmed, and shouting to him to go back.

Now, it must be remembered that none of them knew what had happened on the plateau, so not for an instant did it occur to them that the Tiger was a fugitive. On the contrary, they supposed that either by luck, or by judgement beyond their understanding, he had deliberately aimed to intercept them. And when a yelling horde of Indians and half breeds appeared round the bend higher up the steps, it only tended to confirm this. That the Indians were, in fact, pursuing the Tiger, did not occur to them. There was no reason why it should.

The Tiger pulled up when he saw the three white men in front of him. He threw a nervous glance over his shoulder, although this gave the impression that he was waiting for his men to come to his assistance. The situation appeared critical.

Algy addressed the Tiger. "Get back," he ordered. "Get back and tell those men of yours to stop, or I'll shoot you."

The Tiger appeared not to understand. He shouted something, either in Spanish or in a local dialect. Anyway, none of those below him knew what he said. Then he did a surprising thing. He looked up, then down the steps. Then he surveyed the face of the cliff. Before any of the watchers suspected his intention, with a cat-like leap he reached a narrow ledge above the path, a ledge that was not visible to those below. Along this ledge he made his way towards the hole from which the comrades had just emerged.

At first Algy thought he simply intended getting above them, but as soon as he realised what he was going to do, he shouted a warning. Again, either the Tiger did not understand or he took no notice. He disappeared into the hole.

He was out of sight only a moment or two. Then he reappeared, screaming, snatching and striking at a number of black hairy objects that were running over his body. He appeared to forget where he was, so it came as no surprise to the horrified watchers when he lost his balance

154

and fell. He landed head first on the stairway amid a shower of rocks, and there he lay, limp in unconsciousness.

For a second or two Ginger stared blankly at the wretched man, his brain trying to keep pace with events. As in a dream he saw Algy bring his heel down viciously on a loathesome great spider, and shuddered. Then, remembering the Tiger's men, he looked up the steps and saw with fresh astonishment that they had stopped. One man now stood a little way in front of the others. It was a white man, in spotless ducks. He blinked and looked again. "I'm going crazy," he muttered.

Algy, looking rather pale, swung round. "What are you talking about?" he snapped.

Ginger pointed. "Is that Carruthers, or am I beginning to imagine things?"

Algy stared. He passed his hand wearily over his forehead. "It's Carruthers, all right," he said. "If he's here, then Biggles shouldn't be far away."

"I don't get it," muttered Eddie in a dazed voice.

"Something seems to have happened while we were away," murmured Algy.

Then Carruthers raised his hand in greeting, and shouted: "What are you fellows standing there for? Come on up. We were wondering where you were. It's all over."

Algy turned a stupefied face to Ginger. "Did you hear that?" he said incredulously. "It's all over."

"What's all over?" demanded Ginger, whose nerves were beginning to crack.

"Let's go up and find out," suggested Algy.

They went slowly up the steps. Carruthers went on ahead of them. They could hear him shouting. By the time they reached the top Biggles was standing there.

"What do you fellows think you're playing at?" he inquired curtly.

"Playing!" snorted Algy. "Playing! That's pretty good." He laughed bitterly.

"I told you to wait until I came back."

"So we should have done if somebody hadn't blown the place up."

155

"What happened to the Tiger?" asked Biggles.

Algy told him. "Some of the slaves are carrying him back up here," he concluded.

Biggles nodded. "That saves us a lot of trouble," he observed. "Let's go and meet him. I want to get that map. It should be in his pocket."

"If you're thinking about the treasure you won't need it," said Ginger with relish.

"Why not?"

It was Ginger's turn to smile. "Because we've found it."

Biggles started. "So that's what you've been up to, is it? I might have guessed it. Well, let's go and have a look at it."

"You can have a look at it—provided I can get to it again—when I've had a look at a square meal and a cake of soap," promised Algy.

Biggles smiled. "That's a fair proposition," he agreed. "Come on, I think we can fix you up."

He led the way back to the machine, leaving Carruthers to attend to the business of sorting out the people on the plateau.

The rest of the story is soon told.

After a meal and a general clean-up, during which time Biggles ran over his adventures and the others gave him an account of what had happened during his absence, they all returned to the underground chamber. They wasted no time searching for the secret spring that actuated the idol, but with crowbars brought from the tool-store forced the panel open. The treasure was then carried into the open, where it could more easily be examined, and where Carruthers officially took possession of it in the name of the Crown.

It proved to be of even greater value than they had supposed, for there were some wonderful jewels, mostly rubies and emeralds, mixed up with the gold. It was a wonderful find, for many of the objects were unique examples of the craftsmanship of the early inhabitants of tropical America, and as such were likely to bring high prices from collectors of such things. As a matter of detail,

156

most of the pieces later found their way into museums, the comrades, including Eddie, receiving a fair percentage in cash of the total sum they produced.

After the treasure had been examined it was taken to the *Wanderer* for transportation to the coast; and as their task was finished, the comrades flew straight back, taking Carruthers and the still unconscious King of the Forest with them. They stayed at the acting-Governor's bungalow while the official inquiry into the whole affair was held. The court, having heard the evidence, exonerated them from all blame in connection with the deaths of the leading conspirators, and unofficially congratulated them on their work in putting an end to a menace that had long been a scandal in the colony. This was very gratifying, and gave them all that satisfactory feeling of a job well done. The Tiger was still in prison, awaiting trial on several charges of murder—evidence of which had been furnished by the released slaves—when they left the colony, but they had little doubt as to what his fate would be.

The formalities over, Eddie, after trying in vain to persuade the others to go with him, returned to the United States. Dusky was given a responsible position in the native police. Then, as there was no reason for them to stay, they climbed once more into the *Wanderer* and continued their interrupted pleasure cruise, well satisfied with the result of their call at the little outpost of the Empire.

THE END

There are many other exciting Biggles books

Here are some of them :

BIGGLES LEARNS TO FLY

The story of how Biggles, at seventeen, joined the Royal Flying Corps and after only fifteen hours of solo-flying went to war.

BIGGLES IN THE BALTIC

Biggles takes a secret squadron to a rocky island in the Baltic. Their deadly mission—to harry the Germans behind enemy lines.

BIGGLES HITS THE TRAIL

A sinister group in the mysterious land of Tibet plan to conquer the world—Biggles, Algy and Ginger help to foil them.

BIGGLES IN THE ORIENT

Hair-raising danger awaits Biggles in the jungles of Asia, when he is called in to solve the mystery of a deadly Japanese secret weapon.

BIGGLES FOLLOWS ON

When British soldiers start deserting, Biggles finds himself hot on the trail of his arch-enemy, Von Stalhein— a trail that ends in a desperate raid on a secret military base on the far side of the world.

Armada

From Alfred Hitchcock,
Master of Mystery and Suspense—

A thrilling series of detection and adventure. Meet The Three Investigators – Jupiter Jones, Peter Crenshaw and Bob Andrews. Their motto, "We Investigate Anything", leads the boys into some extraordinary situations – even Jupiter's formidable brain-power is sometimes stumped by the bizarre crimes and weird villains they encounter. But with the occasional piece of advice from The Master himself, The Three Investigators solve a whole lot of sensational mysteries.

1. The Secret of Terror Castle
2. The Mystery of the Stuttering Parrot
3. The Mystery of the Whispering Mummy
4. The Mystery of the Green Ghost
5. The Mystery of the Vanishing Treasure
6. The Secret of Skeleton Island
7. The Mystery of the Fiery Eye
8. The Mystery of the Silver Spider
9. The Mystery of the Screaming Clock
10. The Mystery of the Moaning Cave
11. The Mystery of the Talking Skull
12. The Mystery of the Laughing Shadow
13. The Secret of the Crooked Cat
14. The Mystery of the Coughing Dragon
15. The Mystery of the Flaming Footprints
16. The Mystery of the Nervous Lion
17. The Mystery of the Singing Serpent
18. The Mystery of the Shrinking House
19. The Secret of Phantom Lake
20. The Mystery of Monster Mountain
21. The Secret of the Haunted Mirror
22. The Mystery of the Dead Man's Riddle
23. The Mystery of the Invisible Dog
24. The Mystery of Death Trap Mine
25. The Mystery of the Dancing Devil
26. The Mystery of the Headless Horse

Armada

has a whole shipload of exciting books for you

Armadas are chosen by children all over the world. They're designed to fit your pocket, and your pocket money too. They're colourful, exciting, and there are hundreds of titles to choose from. Armada has something for everyone:

Mystery and adventure series to collect, with favourite characters and authors . . . like Alfred Hitchcock and The Three Investigators – The Hardy Boys – young detective Nancy Drew – the intrepid Lone Piners – Biggles – the rascally William – and others.

Hair-raising Spinechillers – Ghost, Monster and Science Fiction stories. Fascinating quiz and puzzle books. Exciting hobby books. Lots of hilarious fun books. Many famous stories. Thrilling pony adventures. Popular school stories – and many more.

You can build up your own Armada collection – and new Armadas are published every month, so look out for the latest additions to the Captain's cargo.

Armadas are available in bookshops and newsagents.

Armada